I'LL D? T? THAT!

BY
ALEXANDER NILES

CARTOONS BY
DENNIS EDMUNDS

P.E.P.

Published by: P.E.P. Ltd.
St. Leonard's Mead, St. Leonard's Hill,
Windsor. Berkshire. SL4 4AL.
First published in Great Britain 1996.
© Alexander Niles.
Humour.
ISBN 0 9525920 1 0.
Printed and bound in Great Britain
by Biddles Ltd. Guildford and
Kings Lynn.
Layout and design by P.E.P. Ltd.
Cartoons by Dennis Edmunds.

INTRODUCTION

Something fresh and light-hearted to amuse you. My intention in writing this book is to convey more understandable knowledge to you in a light easy manner. In saying this, I hope it will interest you enough to discuss its topics and gain experience from its advice.

The cartoonist, Dennis Edmunds has a brilliant understanding of the script and has produced a wonderfully humorous pictorial account of its contents.

I set out to try and describe the workings of the EU and became so convinced, in doing so, that it is so bad for Britain, I increased the EU content to over fifty pages.

It is a book campaigning for change and as such I have called upon other sources to project and illustrate my writing. There are two authors whom I would like to thank, first for their courage in exposing the sham of European unity, and secondly for sharing with us their very helpful knowledge. I refer to Monsieur D'Aubert and his book on France in Europe, and the ex-Eurocrat Bernard Connolly with his book 'The Rotten Heart of Europe'. He dared to expose inner secrets of the bureaucratic administration of the EU and consequently lost his job. For their contribution to the debate we must be thankful.

Lastly, if you have enjoyed the humour of this book and have a story to tell yourself, domestic, political, or highly sensitive, I would welcome your contribution to produce a book using readers experiences. So if you can send me stories about your pet absurdities I will try and collate them into a book like this.

I hope you will be entertained by these pages and humour and beauty continue to fill your life.

ACKNOWLEDGEMENTS

Thanks to everyone who contributed their experience to this book. To my Daughter Christabel and Ben, who spent hours proof reading. To my wife for all her help and support and to the beauty and humour that influences me. A very big accolade must go out to my computer expert, Mike Papo, who has overcome all my problems and scanned the cartoons so expertly. To him I dedicate this book. Last but by no means least to Chad for his contributions.

I'LL DRINK TO THEM

Beauty itself doth of itself persuade the eyes of men.

The Rape of Lucrece.   William Shakespeare.

Schemes of political improvement are
very laughable.

Samual Johnson 1709-1784.

GOVERNMENT

During our lives the majority of us lead a dreary existence being governed. For just a moment stop and think what that means precisely: who governs us?, where do they place their power to enact government?, when it all goes wrong, which it does most frequently, who ends up paying the bills while government goes off on yet another tangent? That's Us Folks!

Yes, by abstaining from reaction, we are the poor sheep that allow this strange monster, sold to us as government, to walk over our bodies, trampling us down as it goes.

It spends our last penny and then has the gall at the end of it all to tell us how well it has done, adding how dangerous, stupid, irresponsible and incapable the other side would be if it had gained power.

The truth is there is little to choose between them. Consider this simple act of government and you will see behind the screens. It exposes the real logic of government to create something totally irrelevant that spirals in cost when handed to the dreaded Civil Service. Needless to say, it ends up with their hands in our pockets to pay for their follies.

We can marvel at the off-hand manner adopted when dealing with the third group, except at election time.

THE SIGNPOST

The governing of a country is rather like a sign in the middle of a field that reads:

"DO NOT THROW STONES AT THIS SIGN"

The politician is the sign itself.
The civil servant is the one who erected the sign.
The elector is the poor silly bugger who doesn't know what it means.
The first two groups depend almost entirely on the third group's confusion.
The first group insists that the sign represents a democratic choice.
The second group knows that this is nonsense but is prepared to go along because they painted the logo.
The first group think that the logo is good and claims it as a first for themselves.
The third group scratches its head.
The first group spend much time arguing which way the sign should face.
The second group couldn't care less so long as it stays where it is.
The second group have an idea that the sign needs its support pole painted.
The first group pretends to be horrified at the cost but agrees just so long as it still faces the right direction.
The third group scratches its head.

The first group becomes excited and suggests that another sign be erected alongside stipulating the size and shape of the stone that must not be thrown at the sign.

The second group wholeheartedly concurs, happily informing the first group that the extra cost will be provided by the third group.

The third group scratches its head.

The second group have the additional sign erected and then put up another that explains the reason for the first, and the second, and the current one.

The first group have apoplexy screaming that the third sign was done without their authority.

The second group have an explanation.

The first group accepts it.

The third group stops scratching its head and strokes its nose.

Time passes and the first group appeals to the third group for re-election.

The second group couldn't care less.

The third group scratches its head, its nose, its chin; then it decides.

Suddenly there's a new first group.

The second group couldn't care less.

THE THIRD GROUP GOES BACK TO SCRATCHING ITS HEAD.

The deed of government is seen to be well and truly done. By some!

Lets take a look at an average voter, press-ganged into voting by that fanatical breed, the party worker.

Us human beings (that's Us Folk) are also governed, and although we profess to be an advanced race, follow the practices of sheep when it comes to voting. That is to say MOST of us.

Consider a polling station on election day and seventy-nine year old Martha has been collected by a nice man in a car so she can vote. Martha gave up thinking about politics twenty years ago but, because a smooth talking party worker persuaded her to put a poster in her window, she felt obliged. Martha was also confused. She was at the old village hall where her late husband had been the caretaker for many years.

It was not as she remembered it. The assembly hall was divided into sections. At one side of the hall there was a table behind which sat three people: two very smart ladies wearing dresses which Martha could never afford and a man with a bow tie. The man that had driven the car ushered Martha towards the table.

Without looking up the bow tie said,

"Name?"

Martha leaned, a little tired, on her walking stick and remained silent.

Bow tie raised his eyes.

"I asked your name, Madam."

Martha straightened her back and, biting back the pain of arthritis, stood erect.

"Young man," she barked, "you do not care who I am almost as much as I do not care who you are. So you can put that in your pipe and light it."

Martha turned away and limped towards the door. The young man that drove the car dashed across the hall and took hold of Martha's arm.

"Are you not going to vote?" he asked.

Martha smiled.

"If I wish to throw peanuts to a load of monkeys who refuse to eat them, I'll vote."

SO ENDED SEVENTY-NINE YEAR OLD MARTHA'S EXPERIENCE OF POLITICS.

Although I always vote, I am tempted to say Martha was not a sheep and was probably right.

If you think these are light-hearted and cynical examples of government just stop and think for a moment. Remember that mess called "Poll Tax." A real life horror story.

Yes, this neat little bit of legislation, in its short existence, caused riots in the streets. It saw MPs go to jail rather than pay. It also dethroned the Queen of governments and proved un-adaptable to economic collection. The crunch was that it cost a prohibitive amount to collect and caused blockages in the courtrooms up and down the country.

Who foots the bill for all this folly? Well, government created the poll tax, the civil service enacted the bill: yes, you are catching on fast: we pay. It's so easy, so expensive, so unfair.

The government move on to a mark two poll tax: community charge, call it what you will. The best thing since sliced bread we are told. "It's good for us." What they mean by "us" is the government.

Again we are suckered with the cost of closing down the old tax, including unpaid bills and the octopus of civil servants and computers especially employed on administrating its wasteful collection. The cycle repeats itself again with the new tax. This clearly illustrates the mind of government that is never at a loss to find new ways of extracting our hard earned cash. For pure gall it should get an Oscar.

Finally, local governments in many areas have levied a surcharge on poll tax bills to cover the shortfall by non-payers. Thus those that do abide by the law get clobbered again for those that don't. Unfair? It sure as hell it is.

I AM A MOUSE THAT LIVES IN A HOUSE.

THAT'S OFFICIAL.

My letter box rattled and a brown envelope with a cellophane window hit the floor. Brown envelopes with cellophane window are always bad news. Anyway I'd had a good night's sleep and my hangover wasn't yet in full gallop, so I opened it.

Four hundred and ninety quid it said and lets have the money.

I suppose it was curiosity that had provoked them into breaking down what I thought was half the council's annual income; police, dustbin men, lighting, etc. I decided to telephone them;

Brrrrrr---Brrrrrr-----Brrrrrr---Brrrrrr--Click.

A voice, speaking something between Latin and Serb-Croat told me that the office was unattended and offered the suggestion that I call back at two.

Giving them reasonable time to settle back to work I called back. I was unceremoniously handed from one person to another till either the loser of the draw got me or they ran out of options. I pointed out that there must be some mistake as I had already received my poll tax bill and had arranged with my bank to pay monthly instalments.

The voice of authority on the other end assured me that that was impossible as the first and only bill was sent out that very week.

I was about to protest further when I noticed the address on the bill was different to mine.

"Oh," I said, "now I can see the error. You are billing me for a house in Market Street but I don't live there, I live in Chestnut Avenue."

The authority, as if expecting this reply, retorted;

"You have a shed in Market street beside the allotments which you recently modified after obtaining planning permission. You excavated the site, put down a concrete base and erected a larger shed. Due to the concrete base and the larger floor area this now falls into the planning zone of habitable buildings and therefore carries a poll tax rating."

"You're joking aren't you?" I replied, thinking he watched too much television. "I keep my tools, fertilisers and rotavator in the shed. No one lives in it unless you class Mickey as a tenant?"

"Now we're getting somewhere," barked the authority, "best to come clean in the long run. If you would kindly furnish us with full details of your tenant we won't bother you again."

I put the phone down in dumbfounded shock. This moron of authority didn't know Mickey Mouse. Then it struck me. I hadn't stated he was a common mouse who had taken up residence in my shed. I had named him Mickey because of his big ears and his saucy grin.

Suddenly a thought struck me. I put pen to paper and wrote a polite letter to the authority advising them that all further bills should be sent to Mickey as he had taken up residence in my shed in Market Street.

Do you know I have not been bothered by demands?

However my shed has had some nasty letters posted to it for Mickey. The other day I saw two burly men, looking like bailiffs, scratching their heads and laughing about their latest mission.

Today I received the penance for my deceit. A surcharge bill for all poll tax payers to compensate the council for all residents that had failed to pay their bill. It was worth every penny of the thirty-eight pounds supplement. Mickey has now settled down and had a large family. I am leaving him to fill in the necessary forms for the council in future.

———————

Now let's look at the composition of government. Simply, it consists of those in power on one side and those that think they should be in power on the other. Thus they are able to play a game called 'Point Scoring' all day long, bobbing up and down, expounding their opinions on a less than attentive audience; then sitting down with satisfaction written all over their faces remonstrating that they have, 'Got one over,' the opposition.

Occasionally a minister will get up and make a profound statement. The opposition shadow minister will rubbish it and the members of both sides will vie to add their tuppence worth for recorded history.

Once a day the prime minister will be available for questioning. Most of the questions from his side are aimed at highlighting himself or his ministers and their achievements leading into what his commitments for the day involve. This is a daily insight into the life of a leader.

It has become a custom to cram as much into this space as possible, so the present leader can look at least half as busy as the workaholic lady that preceded him. In reality he is watching a recording of his favourite football or cricket moments for most of the evening.

The opposition leader's job is to quickly and decisively neutralise any success the government might claim, especially if it is a resounding success. This applies even if it is a policy promoted by the opposition in the past. He will use political jargon as an economist uses statistics. This tactic clouds success and confuses Us Folks.

This is largely the reason we never seem to have unchallenged success anymore. Perhaps this contributes to our feeling of inferiority.

The floor of the house is but a rubber stamp for the back-room boys who assemble plans and formulate the endless legislation that is churned through the sausage machine. Committees vet them. Interested parties feed in their usually blinkered and narrow-minded thoughts. The back-room boys ignore most approaches to mould policy their way, leaving in its wake a host of disgruntled interested parties.

When the bill is finally passed, not forgetting the other (non representative) House of Lords, it goes to the civil service to enact within the law. Immediately it is changed out of all recognition from the bill that went through the wing politique.

It takes upon itself an air of mystique. Written in gobbledy-gook it is only comprehended by top civil servants and complete morons. It does this for three main reasons.

1. simplicity is frowned upon by the civil service, whose motto is, "why make something easy when with a little effort you can make it unintelligible?"

2. By making it incomprehensible the civil service can do almost whatever they like with it.

3. To employ more civil servants to untangle the mess it creates and perpetuate the cancerous growth of the monster civil service.

All three are good reasons in the eyes of the service, but ultimately end up in higher taxes to pay for the extravagances of the servants of government.

At this point a very wise saying should be noted; 'Beware of beginnings'. This should be a compulsory recitation every morning for all politicians and civil servants.

THE FETE OF DEBATE.

The House of Commons is an impressive piece of architecture and is a tribute to the lead in both Christopher's pencils at the time of its conception. Alas, the MP's that occupy this grand building don't seem to be capable of reflecting the splendour in which they work.

An American friend of mine came to England determined to spend a couple of months experiencing London.

"There's a public gallery at the House of Commons," he said to me, "can you get me in?"

"I can get you in," I told him, "the only trouble is keeping you awake long enough to afford you an experience." He insisted, so I arranged it and we found ourselves sitting in the gallery staring down onto the area where the laws of the land are passed. The same area where over 600 elected members, in the name of democracy, thrash out problems of international, national and local importance: problems that are the concern of every parent of every baby kissed by every candidate during an election.

It was four o'clock in the afternoon and my friend had a question:

"Where the hell is everybody?"

"Oh, you don't find many visitors at this hour," I told him.

"I'm not talking about visitors. I'm talking about politicians."

I looked down onto the floor of the House of Commons and counted the members sitting on the benches. I'd had more people at a small dinner party.

"Pretty slack at this time of day," I told my friend.

"Pardon me?"

"Well you know, sort of a quiet time."

Just at that moment, one member on the right side of the House stood up and began to shout about something. They always shout in the House of Commons for reasons best known to themselves.

It became apparent, from his first utterance, that the honourable gentleman was talking on a matter of national importance, namely the fate of the British Banger.

"The honourable gentlemen opposite will concur with me that the fate of the British Banger, threatened by the mindless bureaucrats from Brussels, is of the utmost importance to the future of our great country. It is indeed a matter of pride that I stand today in support of such a great institution developed by our forefathers in industry to create one of our greatest achievements for mankind."

"Is this gentleman for real? Does he believe all that crap?" asked my friend.

"No. He is building up for what is a game of point-scoring. Wait and see," I replied.

"It is with great anger that I heard the Brussel's bureaucrats are planning to prohibit the word 'sausage' unless the meat content of same is over seventy percent. I feel, and I am sure I can speak for you all when I say, this is an insult to the very foundation of our industry. Haven't they got anything better to do than undermine the institutions that have made Britain great?

I call upon you all to censor their action and instruct our Euro MP's to veto this unwarranted attack on our national assets."

Upon this burst of patriotism the member sat down to a half hearted chorus of, "Here here's," mumbles, and assorted snores dotted around the sparsely attended chamber.

At first the next speaker, high up on the far left, was not even apparent to the Speaker, when it was established that he was standing, not sitting, he was allowed to proceed:

"The honourable gentleman has brought to our attention a matter of great importance to the working class families of Britain. The Banger has long been part of our staple diet and a symbol of the struggle by the working class. I must say that the framework that surrounds the history of the Banger has been ignored by the government. I refer of course to the scandalous conditions which exist up and down the country in the banger factories of Britain. The low wages and the long hours the workers have to endure is nothing short of a national scandal. It is time that minimum working wages were set in conjunction with maximum working hours, to reduce the frustration felt by our heroic comrades in the front line. I move that these conditions are brought into any agreement proposed to the EU commission."

My friend looked puzzled. "All this fuss over a simple sausage. Surely the last speaker should have supported the first for national honour's sake?, putting aside his irrelevant issues?"

"My friend, this is point scoring. That is what this whole place is about. It's a game that keeps them happy."

At that moment a junior Minister was on his feet and about to reply to the debate.

"Mr Speaker; honourable members; I have just returned from Brussels, having negotiated a bilateral agreement with the commission, which I think will

18

answer your fears and solve the possibility of an international incident. I speak of course about the fate of the British Banger.

I have reached a compromise with the EU commission that will allow us to continue to serve our national Banger, provided we do not attempt to market it in Europe. As compromise is the best way ahead, I am sure you will welcome this news."

A stunned silence followed, surprising the junior minister who expected applause. However, he eventually sat down awkwardly.

My friend exclaimed; "Surely that is a defeat? Your sausages can't be marketed in Europe."

"Not in the eyes of the British. The politicians have saved another super myth. A corner-stone of Britain, they would say, exaggerating as usual. The voters, Us Folk, can stick to the diet we know. Everyone is happy."

"What about the free market exports and the balance of trade?"

"Oh, the manufacturers will make a Eurobanger for export no doubt extolling the virtues of high meat content, so everyone is satisfied."

"It sure is a strange system you run here. Surely the first speaker should have known the result of the junior minister's visit, so why the debate?"

"Of course he did. That's called check mate. He led the opposition into a trap and the minister performed the check mate. It's team work. That's the game called point scoring."

As we left the visitor's gallery and happened, by mistake, to pass the MP's dining area, I couldn't help noticing the speciality of the day: BANGERS AND MASH.

Government is composed of MP's representing constituencies. It is elected by Us Folk after a thing called an election. To win the day, lies and half truths are mixed with an ingredient of promises not to be fulfilled, exaggerations, and scare stories about their opponents.

This is preceded by six months of interest cuts, tax cuts, increase in the house building programme, reduction in unemployment, increase in road construction with a similar performance in hospital and school building programmes. This is a ploy by the sitting government to buy votes. It helps to confuse Us Folk and give at least a five percent advantage to the sitting government party. However, no matter who gets into power Us Folk will be sure to foot the bill for at least the next three years.

This is all done because the party in power can rely on short memories to forget the pure misery of the last three years.: hence the saying, 'A week in politics is a long time'. To govern, the party must have an overall majority in the house or be able to call on the support from a minority party to form a coalition. The latter is a rarely used practice.

What are the qualities required to become a successful M.P.?

Well, first you must blindly follow your party line, even when you know that it is wrong. Parties do not like and will not tolerate dissent or public argument.

Furthermore, following on from this, you must have no opinions, flushes of conscience, or principles, except those that govern your party. When you reach ministerial level you must not disclose anything you find out that worries your mind which should be public knowledge. If you do disclose government secrets you could get cracked like the egg lady at the Ministry of Health. She was an honest person. She cared for the people, Us Folk, enough to risk her career to put right what she considered the concealment of a health hazard to the public.

She paid the ultimate price by so doing at the hands of a party that seemed intent on hiding important matters of national concern from Us, the blinkered Folk. The reason of course is that government wish to hide the administration blunders by civil servants and ministers. They portray it as protecting the public: how patronising.

In short a successful M.P. has to be untrue to their principles; flexible enough to walk the tightrope of decision, circumvent direct answers to any question, and turn a question into a winning party point. They have to be able to claim success for something they did not do, turn a disaster into a success story for media mileage, and vote with the party regardless. It seems an easy qualification to obtain a thirty two thousand pound salary: if you have no conscience, that is.

The following snapshot shows a typical party meeting of the local executive choosing a candidate.

THE CANDIDATE

Mr. Able was a mature man in every sense. Up to now his life had been full of successes. In his school days he gained entry to Oxford with four straight A's in English, Economics, French and Sociology. He had a compelling interest in people and wanted to help improve the lives of the socially deprived. Therefore, at university he majored in Sociology and gained honours.

From there he had spent five years attaining experience in the field, working first with a psychiatric unit, then as a second in command of a social services office.

It was at this office he really got to grips with the human problems confronting the unfortunate sections of our society, as well as the parasites that leech off anyone that can be suckered. In the three years he was employed by the council, he devised ways of helping the needy and stone walling the others: so much so, he had the nick-name of 'Hitler', amongst the army of Dole Queue Dodgers, most of whom had building site employment or odd jobs as well as being on the dole. He exposed them when he found they had regular jobs.

It was from this stand he thought he had the right qualifications to really change ideas and influence a national effort to help the needy. Indeed his drive and ability were tuned and ready for the big task. That is why he put his name forward for parliament, hoping to steer minds to a better method of helping the poor of our society, while exposing the dodgers.

This was the reason he was sitting with nervous anticipation for his final interview by the select committee that Wednesday. He had passed the first round and was on a short-list of two. His opponent was, in his view, a walk-over.

Mr. Flash was a local business man who had made a fortune out of scrap metal and now wanted the respectability of being a paid politician. The only thing he had ever done locally for the community was to shower the party with cash whenever it ran short.
In the past he had a reputation for thumping people he disliked and had several serious accusations against him for mis-treating his wife. He had power and influence from his wealth.

Mr. Able was convinced that as long as he presented himself in a forthright manner his qualifications would win the day against Mr. Flash with all his wealth.

The door opened and Mr. Able was ushered into the room. The Chairman of the party sat in the centre surrounded by the Aldermen, Counsellors, the Agent and a man from head-office. Sitting at the side were five men and two women he had never seen. The Chairman opened the interview by welcoming him and congratulating him on reaching the short list. Then he was simply asked why he wanted to become a MP.

This was his opportunity to impress. He gave them a short account of his experience and then developed his knowledge into a policy. Backing each point he made with examples of success he had achieved. It was obvious to anyone present he knew his subject well and his account was both precise and informative. He took care not to speak too long but filled his dispatch with illustrated examples supporting his thinking.

Then the committee in turn asked individual questions on his reaction to policies. Luckily they did not touch on matters in which he had variance with party thinking, so he presented his reply satisfactorily. Next he was asked if he was to disagree with the party at anytime, how would he vote?

He thought a moment. As it was a general question it afforded a general reply, ignoring the area where his conscience would not, on any account, allow a deviation from principles. Undoubtedly, this was an important question. So he replied:

"I would argue my corner in committee and if I was out-voted I would concede to the party's majority view. If it was a matter not in committee I would consult my local constituency before voting."

This seemed to satisfy the assembled members. The chairman came back with the sting. "Let's get more specific. If you were asked to bring back hanging, how would you vote?"

Able released an invisible sigh and answered:

"I would apply my rule as I have already outlined." At this point, they turned to domestic and family questions. When he finally left the assembled committee he felt quietly confident that he had done enough to convince them he was the best choice.

He was told he would have to wait till Saturday to know the result. It was going to be a time of nervous anticipation. Like most of us, he did not like waiting!

By chance, his waiting time was halved. At lunch-time Friday, as usual, he had his sandwiches in the office and took the opportunity to catch up with the local news. As he came to the local political section he was struck by shock that quickly changed to anger when he realised the implications of what he had just read.

The article stated that after careful selection his party had chosen a local man Mr. Flash to represent them at the forthcoming election. They were sure he would bring much needed knowledge about local issues to the attention of parliament. Mr. Able was angry because he knew that the local paper went to 'bed', as they call it, on Tuesday, one day before his final interview. It was a sham, a pretence of democracy. Cash had won the day over knowledge and ability.

"That's politics," he sighed, and turned his energy to something worthwhile.

———————

This illustrates how the party system often chooses the wrong candidate for purely financial reasons or union considerations rather than selecting the best man for the job. It is easier to employ a 'yes' man than a man of independent knowledge. So few candidates get ahead in politics who have qualifications for office, like Mr. Able.

POLITICAL STATEMENTS

WHAT THEY REALLY MEAN

"We do not pay much attention to opinion polls."

Meaning: "We only agree with opinion polls when they favour us."

"Although we have failed to hold the seat, given the present circumstances we are surprised the opposition did not do better."

Meaning: "This is a catastrophic result which reflects the mess we have made of government."

"The opposition is redundant of ideas."

Meaning: "They have a point."

"I believe our party's policies will be seen as fair by all people of intelligence."

Meaning: "We have done enough to satisfy the bankers and the main contributors to party funds and the rest aren't intelligent enough to suss us out."

"We have entered a period of economic decline and we must all tighten our belts in an effort to overcome our problems."

Meaning: "We have made a complete mess of the economy so you must suffer. We will naturally expect our salaries to increase at double the rate of inflation."

"Education is safe in our hands."

Meaning: "No change in a mediocre system."

"Education must change to the progressive method."

Meaning: "Education will get progressively worse as we can't afford proper teachers."

"Education needs more qualified teachers."

Meaning: "Some of the teachers we have are an unqualified bunch of anarchists."

OUR FALTERING LEADERSHIP

Has leadership by example died? By the blistering repetition of cases where leaders hang on to office when their credibility has been brought into question I have to admit, leadership by example is all but dead. Unfortunately respect for leadership has been killed by starvation of example.

It may sound petty to suggest leaders should abide by a set code of practice but they are in a high position and our conduct will depend on their attitude to their responsibility.

Today, unfortunately we can cite so many cases where leaders should have resigned but instead clung on to their office.

The Rt. Hon. Nigel Lawson, as Chancellor of the Exchequer, presided over a considerable fall in the pound caused by incorrect action in releasing the monetary clamps too soon and letting the money supply go free. This grave error wiped millions of pounds off UK Ltd., Us Folk's money. At this point he did not do the honourable thing and resign. He waited till he had a policy row with Mrs. Thatcher and then resigned. His reward was knighthood and a directorship of Barclays Bank.

The Rt. Hon. Norman Lamont, through hesitation and bad advice, lost UK Ltd. billions of our hard earned money on Black Wednesday, while speculators like Soras milked the system for all its worth. This was the largest fall in assets for UK Ltd. in its recorded history. He did not resign and had to be pushed out in the end.

The governor of the Bank of England, Mr. Leigh Pembleton, through muddled thinking and inaction, it was said, did not read correctly what was happening on Black Wednesday and accordingly had to spend a fortune from the reserves to cover the situation: Us Folks money in his charge. Did he resign? Did he hell. He went on till retirement and was awarded the honour of Lord for his services. It seems to pay these days to hang on regardless! In the view of Us Folk, it proves once more that honours mean nothing, just a sop for the 'jobs for the boys' club.

Black Wednesday was not the only scandal during his time in the bank. His leadership failed to deal with the BCCI fraud until the position was highlighted in the national press forcing the bank into action. Leigh Pembleton's office received a report, outlining the fraud taking place, two years before the eventual collapse.

Lord King, of British Airways, presided over a scandal involving illegal action against a rival airline, Virgin Atlantic. He constantly denied he knew anything about it but every piece of evidence showed it was a policy from the top. It is inconceivable he did not know and it is most likely he ordered the action. Did he resign when it was made public? No he didn't. However, due to consistent pressure he retired early when he had made sure his policies were in safe hands.

So what does it take to make a leader resign for honour? A lot, it seems.

The latest sad spectacle of clinging onto office has been the result of the Scott report. How two ministers,

so criticised, could continue in office is beyond my belief. Is it any wonder the population in general and Us Folk in particular have no respect anymore for politicians and can trust none of them further than we can spit?

We will not get back to successful leadership till we get less greed from the top, in their constant excessive wage increases and bonus allotments, and return to leadership by example, which includes wage restraint.

It is interesting to study how the population is gainfully employed. Statistics from government reports bring you a startling presentation.

I'M TIRED

Yes, I'm tired. For several years I've been blaming it on middle age, poor blood pressure, lack of vitamins, air pollution, saccharin, obesity, dieting, underarm odour, yellow wax build up, and a dozen maladies that make you wonder if life is really worth living.

But I find out t'aint that.

I'm tired because I'm overworked.

The population of this country is fifty-one million; twenty-one million are retired. That leaves thirty million to do the work. There are nineteen million in school. That leaves eleven million to do the work. Of this total, two million are unemployed, and four million are employed by government.

That leaves five million to do the work.

One million are in the armed forces, which leaves four million to do the work.

31

From that total, three million are employed by county and borough councils, leaving one million to do the work.

There are sixty-two thousand people in hospitals, and nine-hundred and thirty-seven-thousand nine hundred and ninety-eight in prisons.

That leaves two people to do the work.

You and me.

And YOU are sitting on your arse reading this.

No wonder I'm bloody tired.

To conclude, government should adopt a policy of invisible control over the nation's affairs from the present media-led domination of every aspect of our lives. Government should not dictate our lifestyle but complement it.

THE MONARCHY IN MODERN SOCIETY

The Queen is the constitutional head of our nation, above politicians. She is also head of the Church of England; as such she commands great theoretical power if she so wished to use it.

Our Queen has now reigned for four decades and in this time has seen the evolution and occasionally rapid change in her domain. In all this time, the Monarch, as head of the Commonwealth of Nations and Queen of England, has stabilised a grouping that did not always see eye to eye.

No politician could have achieved this. The reason is that the Queen is above politics, unlike a president who is elected through the political system.

In this long reign she has sacrificed her own personal life for the good of our nation and for this sacrifice I, for one, wholeheartedly thank her. I do not know one other person who would willingly take on this task for all the wealth attributed to the Royal household. So why is there so much talk in the Nation about the future of the Monarchy?

I suspect it has three main reasons. One is already reformed; taxation of the royal purse. I hope this will be applied so it is seen to be even-handed and not taxation of assets by choice.

Criticism of her close advisers is also justifiable as they continue to maintain out of date protocol in a modern world. Us folk do not wish to be totally subservient. It is not in step with the modern practice. Care should be taken to re-think the formalities of protocol and the Royal contact with the public, and stop old-fashioned requirements such as deep curtsies by ladies, sometimes barely able to do so because of their age and physical condition. It is grossly demeaning and totally out of keeping to adhere to this practice.

Example is one way Royalty can lead us. Lord knows it is missing in the political arena and in top management today.

Our Queen's example has been faultless. Unfortunately this cannot be said of her children, three of which have married and all are either divorced or separated. This is an unfortunate lead from the top when the divorce rate is higher than ever before and marriage as a stabilising force is in jeopardy. The Queen is, after all head of the Church of England. The greatest threat to our future comes from the change of attitude to family life.

Us Folk desperately need a stable example of family life as a role model to follow and I suspect the future of the monarchy depends on this too.   The absence of example in respect of family life must be a decisive factor in the debate about the future of the Monarchy.

I personally believe that Charles should not succeed to the throne but should pass it on in favour of his eldest son and this should be announced, after consideration, as quickly as possible.

THE EUROPEAN ECONOMIC COMMUNITY

The people of Europe, that includes Us Folk, are increasingly alarmed at the steady flow of policy documents churned out by the citadel of bureaucracy in Brussels.

Cast your mind back to the days of the campaign to win the vote for entry into Europe. You will remember how the "Yes" campaign, led by the Rt. Hon. Edward Heath convinced Us Folk it would be a good idea to be part of Europe.

It made common sense to belong to a group of free traders on our doorstep and the weight of this simple message carried the day against a somewhat muddled and negative "No" campaign led by rebels from both the main parties. The weight of the political clout was behind the "Yes" vote as all three parties officially campaigned for it. So we weighed up the arguments and voted for entry.

Little did we know what we were letting ourselves in for by so doing.

One of the best things the Thatcher government did was to abolish the GLC. It was a useless, bureaucratic organisation that clogged up the decision process of local government by pushing paper from one department to another and backwards and forwards between local councils. It successfully bogged it down in red tape and bureaucratic meddling, never making decisions. It allowed the local authorities to excuse themselves for the lack of action. It was a third layer of heavyweight bureaucratic authority, costing Us Folk, the ratepayers, a fortune, and effectively delaying badly needed actions to keep London working. Very few have missed it except the Empire builders, the bureaucrats and of course the Loony Left. However, the Conservative motivation to disband it was for the wrong reasons. Instead of realising its role of strangling anything it touched through bureaucratic suffocation, it was disbanded because of a political bias aimed in arresting the left wing influence on London.

That caused its execution. Whatever the reason, the result was good for London and a seldom seen victory against useless bureaucracy.

So why is it that all our politicians, in unison for once, want to impose on Us Folk another third tier of government, this time even above our national government that will, if the politicians and bureaucrats get their way, clone all EU countries as one, with one legislator and one EU currency and rules that make us all so monotonously the same.

I suspect, in the case of the politicians, it is another case of very lucrative jobs for the boys at the top, with expense accounts of unequalled proportions. For the bureaucrats it is simply power lust. It is another new avenue to create a monster Empire.

An example of the inefficiency we can expect if the politicians and bureaucrats get their way can be clearly seen in the common agricultural policy. It swallows up around seventy percent of the EU budget and costs

'ERE, WOJJA FINK ABOUT THIS SINGLE CURRENCY, 'ARRY?
RUIN US, SID, IT'LL BLOODY RUIN US
TIMES

every family of four over one thousand pounds a year to administer, yet it goes directly against a free economy by propping prices up artificially and producing farmers that become lazy, and even lie or cheat the system to get subsidies through the administration's lack of investigation. The system has been found to be rife with large organised crime syndicates like the Mafia, claiming for subsidies that are on offer, for fictitious olive groves or vineyards. Such is the system, that they just pay out on most claims without checks, leaving Us Folk to foot the bill.

They also pay out subsidies to farmers to leave land fallow or grow rape. The farmer often chooses rape, as it is a lucrative crop that can be used as cattle feed or be sold to make oils for cooking and even diesel oil, while he gets the same subsidy as if it were fallow. Other by-products from the plant are rope, string and cord. The plant for its anti-social problems should be banned. It seeds itself everywhere and creates terrible pollen troubles for hay fever and asthma sufferers.

If they can't get the agriculture policy right without such a high subsidy to the farmers, while forcing us to pay something like thirty percent more for our produce on top, how can we expect them to get any policy right?

If you study the record of the EU's financial policy the picture is not much better. The Snake, as it was called, or ERM, has proved to be an absolute disaster. The failure of the ERM was highlighted by black Wednesday but its straight-jacket effect on the National Budget proved too much for several economies including our own, when it forced us to act decisively and leave the doomed attempt to level all EU currencies. Our position has improved considerably since we left, showing how the straight-jacket policies from Brussels effectively stifle individual National developments. Our freedom from the Snake and our exemption from the social chapter will prove to be our strength in years to come.

The German economy has led Europe in the past, with universal respect for its durability. Unfortunately for Europe this stabilising factor is at an end. Germany is suffering from a deepening recession, a factor that the Germans have no experience to overcome. This lack of experience is fuelled by the enormous cost of unification for Germany and the influx of refugees from the Eastern block. To add to this, their repressive industrial laws are driving industry out of Germany. These are the very same type of laws that Jacques Delors wishes to impose on the membership countries of the EU. This gross interference in state sovereignty must be defeated if the EU is to achieve the goal it first set itself, namely a cheap free trade area for its members, supplying a large market for the member states and their products.

The ERM is dead. Long live realism. How then, with all the variance between individual National economies, do they expect to run a single EU currency, the ECU, Euro, or what ever they call it, in the foreseeable future? The answer is that they can't, unless they want to create a far larger disaster than Black Wednesday. I will go as far as to predict the collapse of any attempt to impose such a policy, with far-reaching effect on the credibility of the EU. Will the politicians care? No they will not, because they can go on to their next idea, undoubtedly increasing their own wages for failure somewhere along the way, while Us poor Folk are left with the bill.

The ultimate folly of our politicians and the bureaucrats is to aim towards an EU single parliament cloning Us poor Folk into a mass of subservient Euro-sheep without character or National identity. I fervently oppose this horrific idea and I believe the majority of the citizens of Europe would agree. So what can we do to make sure our view is heard and our politicians listen to us and represent us? We must use every opportunity to make our view known.

I support a free trade area within Europe and extending this to the new democratic states of Eastern Europe.

I oppose the policy that projects us towards a single parliament, where every Nation's birthright is subservient to that single parliament.

I oppose movement towards a single currency that will cost Us Folk the remainder of our taxed income to support. I believe a free trade area will do all the policing of trade practices necessary to achieve true competition, provided no National subsidies are permitted. Laws to govern this are already in place. Need for market motivates all industrialists and is the ultimate incentive to compete. EU regulations are already stifling trade, except for countries like France who only honour laws that favour them.

I oppose a movement towards a third layer of bureaucratic extravagance which is not required to run a free trade area and kills incentive. It is so easy to stifle industry with laws, regulations and paperwork. It is much harder for politicians to leave a market free of restrictions to grow and prosper. It is against a politician's nature.

I predict the EU will force our national economy into higher taxes to pay for its crippling bureaucracy. I predict that the largest net contributor to EU funds, Germany, at the equivalent to eight billion pounds, will require a sizeable reduction in their contribution as their economy slides deeper into recession.

I predict the benefits that should come from a free trade area will be swamped by bureaucratic meddling and a maze of regulations that will effectively neutralise the benefits.

I predict Us Folk, the people of Europe, will pay a high bill for all the unnecessary folly, unless we can change the course of our politicians. It is up to Us Folk to make sure we do.

I predict the single currency will fail to materialise, as they will not find a suitable level to introduce it fairly for twelve or more national currencies, but trying will cost us dear.

I predict a black future unless we get it right.

REQUIEM TO A NATIONAL INSTITUTION

It is revered by American tourists, known throughout the world by travellers. A film star with Cliff Richards as a supporting actor, and immortalised in song by Flanders and Swan; the big six wheeler, diesel-engine, ninety-seven horse power, scarlet painted, London transport omnibus is under a death sentence. Yes, our Double Decker bus, a National Institution, is about to die. That is, if the meddling bureaucrats from Brussels have their way.

Yet this bus has been developed through the ages and taken on the challenge each era of transport has thrown at it.

A follow-on from the stage coach, the first models were horse drawn with open tops to accommodate the poorer travellers, as did the stage coaches that preceded them. This great advance in passenger transport in 1887 started a fashion for travel that grew as fast as the technology allowed, giving the passengers a new freedom. By 1891 a battery driven model was launched followed by a version with a tall chimney, belching its vapour into the London streets.

In 1909 the first petrol driven double Decker was put into service.

In 1922, due to competition from trams a roof was fitted to the top deck for a more comfortable ride. London was last to accept this change. The police opposed it as they felt the roof would make the buses unstable. How wrong they were.

The large driver-only buses of today have developed from these humble beginnings.

Europe has never taken up the double Decker concept except for holiday buses, rather favouring the cumbersome bendy bus that is the cause of so many traffic jams around Europe, yet in every way the double Decker equals, if not betters, the European buses.

Firstly, and most importantly, the double Decker takes up half the space on our roads than the bendy bus for the same ratio of passengers.

It is a bus designed for passengers to sit in comfort not stand like the majority of passengers in the European Bendy bus.

The double Decker's safety record in use is second to none. You only have to spend some time at the London transport testing centre in Chiswick to realise how stable the double Decker is in extreme conditions. This illustrates the genius of the design.

So why do the bureaucrats wish to sound the death knell for this widely loved institution? They say they are trying to rationalise design and safety to allow fair competition in Europe for all bus manufacturers. This sounds fair and even reasonable. That's fine, but why must it penalise proved innovative design for a cloned, space wasting, stand up, traffic jamming, snake-like monster?

I have long ago stopped suggesting Eurocrats use common sense in their decisions as they don't seem to have an ounce between the lot of them.

France, Germany and Italy have failed to penetrate certain world markets outside the EU, notably the far East including Malaya, Singapore, Hong Kong and China.

It is very probable the main manufacturers, Mercedes and Mannesmann from Germany, Renault from France and Iveco (Part of Fiat), brought pressure to bear on the EU Commission to adopt new construction and safety regulations that distinctly favour the Bendy bus, while making the double Decker less attractive to the user companies by re-designing the seating safety regulations in favour of standing customers on single deck buses.

The bendy bus manufacturers fully know this would then open up the far East market to their road consuming, passenger unfriendly, Bendy buses.

The EU Commission should be forced to publish all approaches made to them on this subject by participating companies, MEP politicians, and government lobbies.

Till then, we must be excused in thinking, yet again, the Franco-German alliance in the EU is fudging policies to suite their national interests.

This, in my opinion, is a flagrant interference in our internal affairs, aiming to influence trade we obtain outside the EU and as such, is none of the Commissions God damn business. It is also unacceptable interference in our home market. If we want to continue to use our world famous double decrees, what right have the Commission to object, or is there something Ted Heath did not explain?

In the meantime it looks as if we must say to our beloved double Decker omnibus;

R.I.P.
Unless the people, that's Us Folk, tell the EU exactly
what we think of their interference.

THE EUROPEAN UNION

No political act has ever stirred up so much
emotional feeling within its ranks as the Delors dream of
a united Europe with one currency and one parliament.
(strangely the one factor that is always left out of the
debate is language. Maybe it's a hot potato?). It is a
dream that the politicians and the bureaucrats of
Brussels are hell bent on imposing on a less than
enthusiastic Europe.

Why is there so much dissent? Why so much
argument? Why so much mistrust of the real reasons
for monetary and political union? Is it just Us Folk in
Britain? Or is there growing mistrust of the whole
idea? Indeed is it workable, given so many different
economies and so many national differences?

I am going to attempt to change a very complex issue
into an understandable one so you can judge your own
response to a major change in our lives. It is vitally
important that Us Folk make the right decision over the
European issue, because we are the ingredients that
make political systems possible and also influence its
changes by mass representation. This is by far the most
important decision you will make this century to
influence your future.

A European Union was first projected into the
public debate after the Second World War, although
many theorists formulated their own version before this
time.

Churchill himself supported a European Union as a way of ensuring we did not get a repeat of the two previous World Wars. These were centred around Germany's lust for European power imposed on the fragile minds of people suffering badly from the ravages of high unemployment, and the collapse of the Mark.

An Austrian decorator, Adolf Hitler, was a master of using situations to whip up support for his ambitions, while hiding his lust for revenge against the Jews, Gypsies and anyone else who showed dissent.

It was this catalogue of heinous crimes against humanity that condemned Germany to regret their past and do everything they could possibly do to atone for their atrocities.

However, Churchill's idea of a united Europe was aimed to neutralise national opportunism, and Europe, even Germany (post war), decided it seemed to be the right move which would guarantee to neutralise their main fear, nationalism.

So in 1952 the European Community was formed, consisting of a political and economic alliance of the steel and coal industries, followed by the expansion in 1957 to the European Economic Community (EEC), popularly known as the Common Market. Later that year the Euroatom, the atomic energy commission, was formed. At that point six European states were involved: West Germany, France, Belgium, Italy, Luxembourg and the Netherlands. It wasn't till 1974 that Britain, Denmark and the Republic of Ireland joined, and in 1981 Greece and Portugal entered, followed by Spain in 1986.

In 1989 the Eastern block crumbled when Russia opened the Berlin Wall. Shortly after that, in 1991, Czechoslovakia, Hungary, and Poland became associated members, giving them ten years to line up

with the economic conditions required to become full members. Romania followed in 1992.

In 1993 the EU became one market with free movement of goods and capital, and somewhat more controversial, free movement of state members and visitors.

The European court of human rights hears cases referred to them by the Commission where the Commission has failed as an arbitrator. It covers individual's complaints against the State. Sitting in Strasbourg, it has forced Ireland to drop its ban on homosexuality, Germany to cease to exclude extreme left and right members from the civil service, and in the case of Britain, forced us to pay compensation to relatives of terrorists killed in Gibraltar. It was also used to obtain compensation for terrorists or relations in many cases involving IRA violence.

One terrorist even claimed compensation from Britain for a twisted ankle caused by uneven paving stones, and won the case! As this court overrules the national judiciary, we pay up and face laughter from the terrorists.

In January 1993 the European Economic area was started between nineteen EU and EFTA countries, allowing three hundred and eighty million citizens to move and transfer money freely across national borders and to live, study, and work in one or other countries.

The European Free Trade Association (EFTA), founded in 1960 as a response to the EC , now consists of only four members as Britain, Denmark and Portugal left to join the EC.

In 1973 EFTA made a free trade movement agreement with the EC, representing over half the member country's trade.

Like all politically led, and civil servant run organisations, the EC realised to gain further advantage for their community, monetary stability was desirable. This was triggered by the 1974 oil crisis. So by 1979 the European Monetary System was announced amid large movement in floating exchange rates. The central policy was the exchange rate mechanism based on the European currency unit the ECU. Britain, during a run on the pound, came out of the ERM, and after free-fall, recovered to prosper in comparison with the countries held inside it.

It was Jaques Delors, in April 1989 that announced the intention to move towards a single European currency, with a link to full political union and a single European Government.

Three stages were prepared for EMU:

1. All controls on individual Nation's capital flow would end and be replaced by a European central bank. This would regulate money supply in two stages.

2. The central bank (ESCB) would start by regulating money supplies.

3. Exchange rates between member countries would be fixed and a single currency created, taking over the task of all member's central banks.

The European parliament which meets, not in Brussels, but Strasbourg, has over six hundred seats amongst its member states by proportion. At first it was merely consultative but in 1979 it became directly elected and assumed some powers. However, at the moment its powers are limited. They can dismiss the whole commission. They can also reject the community budget.

Full council meetings are held in Strasbourg and most committees meet in Brussels. The secretariat is in yet another location, Luxembourg.

The political divide in 1992 showed 260 seats held by the left, 203 by centre parties, 55 by the right, 20 by Gaulists and 16 by independents. Since this count the last election produced a shock in France where Goldsmith's new party, opposed to the basic concept of the EU, won 13 seats in the parliament and shocked the political balance in France.

The seed of opposition to federalism and the single currency, opposed by Britain, under the Conservatives (but supported by the Labour and Liberal parties), is now spreading, as the realisation that the Delors plan could not only be an unobtainable goal, but a political disaster.

Britain entered the EC in 1974 after lengthy negotiations carried out by Sir Con O'Neill on behalf of the Hon. Edward Heath. To obtain consent from the public, a referendum was held by Harold Wilson, after an ill debated canvas by the pro and anti-factions.

The anti-faction seemed to be an individual rabble with no coherent policy, while the simple message: 'a large market on our doorstep is good for trade', seemed right and won the day. Little was said about currency union and a single European parliament. If it had been the referendum result would have been, I suspect, a firm rejection.

Just released, under the thirty year rule, an insight into the chief negotiator's doubts over Europe have come to the surface and made fascinating reading. Sir Con O' Neill, a Eurocrat himself, had grave foreboding about the hidden agenda of France and Germany building a super state for their own benefit.

Now that is apparent today, but to have advised the government thirty years ago of this event was either a remarkable prediction or, more likely, a cautionary warning from a careful negotiator who had done his homework. The papers are an advisory report to the Prime Minister to put before cabinet. He went on to list his doubts about a European Union but in the end, with an air of reluctance, decided Britain's role was better served inside Europe rather than with a declining Commonwealth. He therefore recommended that we join Europe to try and change its course away from the Federalist ideal (aims that Napoleon and Hitler failed to create) to a simple, free trading area amongst its members.

In a way, more surprising is the book written by a Brussels bureaucrat, himself a senior negotiator in the EU office dealing with the switch to a single currency. His name is Bernard Connelly and his highly sensitive book is, 'The Rotten Heart of Europe'. Having lived with the policy to formulate the single currency, he was very well placed to access it and obtain all the back room manoeuvring that took place. In his book he claims that the single currency was a dangerous con trick. He goes further to claim Jaques Delors led an international plot to oust Mrs. Thatcher from power. She was the loudest voice to stand against his ideal of a superstate with its own parliament and currency. The Delors plan has its member states, through their parliaments, subservient to the superstate.

He claims the single currency, if allowed to develop, would cripple Europe, as the ERM has destroyed economies, and cost individual states millions of jobs.

Connelly sums up the thesis of his book in the following words:

"My central thesis is that the ERM and EMU are not only inefficient but also undemocratic: a danger not only to our wealth but to our freedom and, ultimately, our peace."

He also states:

"The ERM is a mechanism for subordinating the economic welfare, democratic rights and national freedom of citizens of the European countries to the will of political and bureaucratic elites whose power lust, cynicism and delusions underlie the vast majority of those who now strive to create a European superstate."

Tough words indeed, that hold a strong message: beware of Brussels bureaucrats and politicians. A warning we should heed. He has it from the horse's mouth.

As if this isn't proof enough that the EU has gone too far, the retired architect of the single currency leading to federalism, Jaques Delors, has finally admitted that even France and Germany may not meet the strict financial target of reducing their budget deficits to no more than three percent of gross domestic product by the deadline date.

This would leave two options for the EU: to dilute the terms of entry to the EMU which the Bundesbank have already vetoed, or to postpone the starting date which would mean re-negotiating the Maastricht treaty: a process that could take years. The inertia that this would create could even spell the beginning of the end for a discredited European Union.

A third world authority on economy, Sir Alan Walters, a Eurosceptic, has been remarkably accurate in predicting the pattern of events in Europe. As an adviser to Lady Thatcher, in 1984 he predicted that entry to the mechanism of the ERM would lead Britain to devaluation and a re-alignment of European currencies. He was proved right.

He predicted the cost of German reunification would be at least thirty billion pounds a year for five years. He was right, but on the low side with his estimate. The actual figure reached sixty billion a year.

In 1979, to the disgust of the Euro-enthusiasts, he predicted the ERM would fall apart and two years later he argued that if Britain was to join the ERM they would be forced to impose monetary policies that opposed the requirements to cure an economic slump.

This whole prediction came true and forced Britain eventually to leave the Snake (ERM). On all these predictions he was called a loud mouth who didn't know what he was talking about. Time, once again, proved he was right.

He has also predicted that Britain, outside the ERM, would prosper and she is already showing every sign of so doing. All the indicators look good. He stated Britain would recover while most of Europe would go further into recession (because of the straight jacket of the ERM and EMU). He said Britain, given time, could even acquire German and French markets.

Germany, on the other hand, is going deep into recession made worse by the chaotic state of the Soviet Mafia led economy (an important trading area for Germany). It is also nailed down by the cost of reunification at around sixty billion pounds a year and the continual influx of political settlers from the Eastern block.

The West German tax payers are rumbling discontent at the high level of tax demands on their wealth in a time of recession and uncertainty and Kohl is going to find it increasingly difficult to justify his policies, in particular the single currency and political integration.

France in the meantime is in the throws of a massive slump with political rioting and high unemployment. The Franc is going to pay the price, leaving them in a poor position to join the EMU in 1999.

From this catalogue of disaster and uncertainty, how can Europe meet the 1999 deadline for the EMU?

DO WE GET VALUE FOR OUR MONEY?

There are only three net contributors to the Brussel's bureaucracy: Germany, Britain and France. The rest are net receivers. That means that they get back more than they pay out. However, if you take into account all the costs of membership that are hidden from us, you get a different picture. These costs include directives to change our road signs to Euro-standard and re-build our bridges to the same design as required under EU regulations. Each country is in for enormous bills that the authorities keep quiet about so we don't get to know the full cost of membership. I will deal with those costs later.

An MEP costs each country just short of one million pounds a year to sit in the European Parliament. Their record of attendance does not match their high profile cost. Quite often debates are cancelled as they have been unable to reach a quorum. One record shows a French MEP did not register for one session during a whole year. Some only attended once or twice. Ian Paisley only turned up for eighteen sittings out of fifty-eight.

The parliament sits, not in one location, but three. This makes a massive logistics problem for papers and interpreters. The plenary sessions, one week in every month, are held in Strasbourg.

The committee meetings and political group meetings are held in Brussels on the other three weeks.

The civil servants are located in Luxembourg.

So a convoy of civil servants and paperwork travel the three-hundred and fifty miles between the cities. What a waste of money. One quarter of the budget goes

on travelling between cities. Another quarter goes on translation into the nine languages of Europe.

This travelling all came about from a stupid decision made at the Edinburgh summit of 1992 by heads of state that should have known better. This decision will cost us, the tax payers, an extra five-hundred million pounds a year for at least five years to use Strasbourg as a parliament.

Another complex has been constructed in Brussels, costing in estimate upwards of eight-hundred and forty million pounds. In its first year it was only used for ten half days at a cost to Us Folk of one-hundred thousand pounds an hour.

When asked about these absurdities an MEP just brushed it off by saying; "Democracy is expensive." This is sanctimonious rubbish to hide complacency and the desire to ride the gravy train.

Meanwhile they are building a one-thousand one-hundred-and-thirty office parliament in Brussels to house the expanded EU of the future.

In their vast complexes, at the last auditor's internal check, seventeen-thousand items, costing in estimate over five million pounds were missing, including computers, video cameras, and typewriters, to name but a few. So not only do they take our hard earned money to fund this charade but they carelessly lose goods of a great value and no effort is made to halt it.

HIDDEN COST OF THE EU

It seems a popular pastime of the European Court of Human Rights to overturn any decision made in the British courts. No country's justice system has suffered so many reversals as the British and in particular over sensitive state security matters.

They have awarded the relatives of the Gibraltar IRA terrorists forty-thousand pounds in costs against the British government. Who pays that? Yes, you're right, Us Folk.

They ruled that the Spanish fishermen can claim thirty-million pounds from Britain for lost fishing rights while the EU is forcing us to subsidise thousands of our own fishermen to the tune of fifty million pounds to stop fishing. This is a crazy decision that is rubbishing our fishing industry to subsidise the Spanish fleet so far from their shores. Further to this, our inspectors find the Spanish fishermen are constantly cheating with catches and net sizes.

A series of judgements concerning sexual discrimination has increased government spending on pensions by equalising the retiring age and by giving part time workers the same rights as full time workers in pensions and holidays, which will cost taxpayers upwards of fifty billion pounds.

A similar judgement reduced the qualifying age, for free prescriptions, for men, down from sixty-five to sixty years old, costing an extra forty million a year for us taxpayers to find.

A bill to increase maternity pay to European levels, costs us sixty-million a year.

On top of this, Britain contributes three billion a year net to the CAP (Common Agricultural Policy). The cost of the Common Agricultural Policy is estimated at one-thousand pounds per family per year. This is the extra cost by subsidy on food you have to pay thanks to EU membership.

In addition to this is our contribution to EU membership at ten-billion pounds. This is a burden we all have to pay to fund a remote system, outside our sovereign parliament. These decisions should not be imposed on us by a body such as the European Court of Justice, an un-elected body of left wing advocates that take pride in destroying sovereign rights.

At the present level of cost from EU policies projected forward for ten years and adding further interference levels at the same rate as present from Brussels, EU membership will, in estimate, cost each person, that's Us Folk, five thousand pounds a year. A level that none of us can afford. Therefore we should be actively canvassing for less EU interference with our internal affairs or alternatively, leave the EU.

CORRUPTION

To show the extent of corruption inside the EU a Frenchman, D'Aubert, writes how the top countries receiving EU subsidy handouts, such as Italy, (No 1), Spain, and Greece, milk the system by use of corrupt claims, but are honoured by the EU to progress its own appearance of self importance.

One of the most monstrous uses of our taxes, that's our money, Folks, has been the new EU parliament buildings. Its official location was Strasbourg, but secretly it was started in Brussels. It was not till the mayor of Strasbourg kicked up a scene and threatened to expose the corruption, that this came to light. D'Aubert states not to know the political source in Belgium that pulled off this coup but the end result was a bill for one and a half billion pounds. The Strasbourg building was estimated to cost two-hundred and seventy million pounds; about one fifth of the cost of the Brussels palace of political and bureaucratic stupidity.

Fraud most certainly took place but no one in the EU hierarchy will bend to stop fraud.

Every time British ministers tried to raise the issue of fraud within the council of ministers, Jaques Delors would, to public viewing, pick up and start reading a newspaper, showing his lack of interest in solving corruption or even learning how prevalent it was within the organisation. His whole authority must be questioned for this strange action.

D' Aubert's book states how large networks of Mafia extortion operate on the CAP policy (Common Agricultural Policy). A large food industrialist and grain dealer from the Camorra family and was arrested for defrauding the CAP to the extent of eighty-million pounds in 1993 alone, by means of an export scam involving fake export documents for Couscous to Algeria.

That year his company received nearly two thirds of CAP's subsidies for corn. How much of this was non-existent? The EU does very little to check the authenticity of export documents. The result is that corruption has a free rein with our hard earned cash. Remember, some seventy percent of the EU funds are spent to subsidise farmers within the CAP.

The Sicilian Mafia and the Neapolitan Camorra family were linked to the Jean Monet building in Luxembourg where the three thousand commission officials are situated. The EU pay rent on this building to the sum of three and a half million pounds, and it goes to P2 members of the corrupt Masonic lodge, Mafia families and the two Camorra brothers. These brothers bought a large slice of the property company in 1974 and were under investigation in Italy later, following work carried out for the government after the 1980 earthquake in Italy.

The book discloses that the largest net gainer of export subsidies is a Swiss registered company (for tax purposes) owned by a fraudster banned from the USA. His company received three-hundred million pounds in subsidy in 1992. It states fraud is greatest from countries with corrupted political systems like Italy.

In 1989 Greece was fined a small amount by the EU for issuing false custom forms which pretended corn from Yugoslavia was Greek, to obtain subsidies. The minister involved was jailed for three years.

Sixty percent of the officially registered fraud happens in Italy, and they know the extent of fraud, according to D'Aubert. He says the Italian police discover four times as much fraud as the Italian government reports to Brussels.

In 1994 the head of the state agency in Italy, responsible for distributing Italy's three and a half billion pound CAP subsidy, was arrested on suspicion of corrupt collusion with Italy's largest grain dealer, showing how the Scicilian Mafia has penetrated the Italian government.

In Messina, two million litres of non-existent olive oil was put on the market, a fraud involving eighty-nine companies and in excess of thirty businessmen, worth more than ten million pounds.

Italian police found twenty-seven million pounds stolen from the CAP by Mafia controlled companies in Calabria and Sardinia through a grain storage scam. The commission only made a cursory inspection. They were refused entry into the storage area and because a young journalist was killed while investigating the scam, gave in to intimidation and paid up the subsidy on a non existent stock.

Not once has Italy been threatened with withdrawal of subsidy till they put their house in order.

That's Us Folk's money they give to the Mafia without wincing. How could Jaques Delors justify his stance on corruption within CAP?

The agricultural policy has had longer to adjust itself within EU confines than any other policy, as it was one of the first considered priorities. In the time it has existed it has paid homage to inefficient farming methods and subsidised crime with our money. This has effectively made our food bill cost each EU family one-thousand pounds more than necessary per year. They have made no attempt to encourage efficiency and reward it. They have turned a blind eye to fraud. So we must ask the question; If they can't get this relatively simple policy right, how can we expect them to overcome the problems of a single currency or run a single parliament? The answer is; no way must we trust our democracy to this band of self-indulgant pirates.

THE PERKS OF THE MEP

The estimated cost of a MEP to its member country is nine-hundred and twenty-thousand pounds a year. This is four times the cost of a backbench MP from Westminster. There are over six hundred and fifty of them to pay for out of our hard earned money.

Although they get a salary equivalent to a back bench Westminster MP this is only where the gravy train starts. They are given Tax free salaries, over-generous allowances, chauffeur driven cars, and over-generous travel expenses. The parliament has voted itself so many privileges, MEPs rank now along some of our top industrialists, and we all know how THEY behave.

An allowance for an assistant is seventy-two thousand pounds a year; many MEPs don't have one, or they share one, but they still claim.

Twenty-six thousand, four-hundred pounds a year is allowed for free travel in MEPs own country whether it is spent or not.

One-hundred and fifty-five pounds a day is allowed for accommodation while attending meetings. MEPs often sleep in beds provided in their office and pocket the allowance.

British MEPs get four-hundred and twelve pounds forty pence for a London to Brussels return ticket. If they go economy class they can pocket around ten thousand pounds a year. This perk alone nearly reaches the average salary of Us Folk that have to foot the bill.

The EU employs one-thousand five hundred interpreters at a salary of thirty-one thousand pounds a year.

The lobbyists increase these inflated salaries by adding consultancy to the MEP's potential earnings. This brings them a world apart from reality and beyond any requirement from their electorate.

So do our MEP's work their butts off for this gravy train?

Many plenary sessions cannot reach a quorum. Some MEP's don't bother to show up at all. Others attend less than a quarter of the sessions which occupy fifty-eight days in the year.

The situation is not helped by the location of the plenary sessions. They are held one week in the month in Strasbourg. The committee and political meetings are held in Brussels on the other three weeks in the month. Add to this the fact that the bureaucratic headquarters are in Luxembourg and you realise they have built themselves a gigantic logistics problem. This

has escalated the costs to provide a paper in place service.

There is a continual logistic flow of paperwork for meetings between the centres. Paperwork is often found to be in the wrong place thus halting debate. One quarter of the parliament budget goes on logistics and another quarter goes on translations both avoidable if they had a single meeting place and a single language.

The cost of the discredited decision to have Strasbourg as a parliament costs in estimate an extra one hundred million pounds a year, that's Us Folk's money. This was a totally insane decision by heads of state to satisfy France.

The gravy train doesn't stop there. Eurocrats get above average wages, up to one-hundred-thousand a year for the top men. A special rate of tax of eight percent. Disturbance allowance of sixteen percent of salary. Living standard allowance is two point nine percent from Britain. Household allowance of forty-six pounds a day. Cheap mortgages. One-hundred pounds a month child allowance. Two free return flights home each year for the whole family and so on. So the bureaucrats get the same gravy train to ride.

Well, having paid all this good money out are we getting value for money?

Judge for yourself by two separate decisions made by the Euro bureaucracy.

The first hairbrain scheme that is charged to us folk to pay its cost is a directive to rehabilitate prostitutes and give them training for six months for any job they want (MEP?). Then give them a new home (So they can use it for their old trade. Presumably with a no-inspectorate policy in line with other policies). 'Its a crackpot scheme introduced by meddling do-gooders.' said Lord Tebbit. I say it is just another Euro disgrace using our hard earned cash.

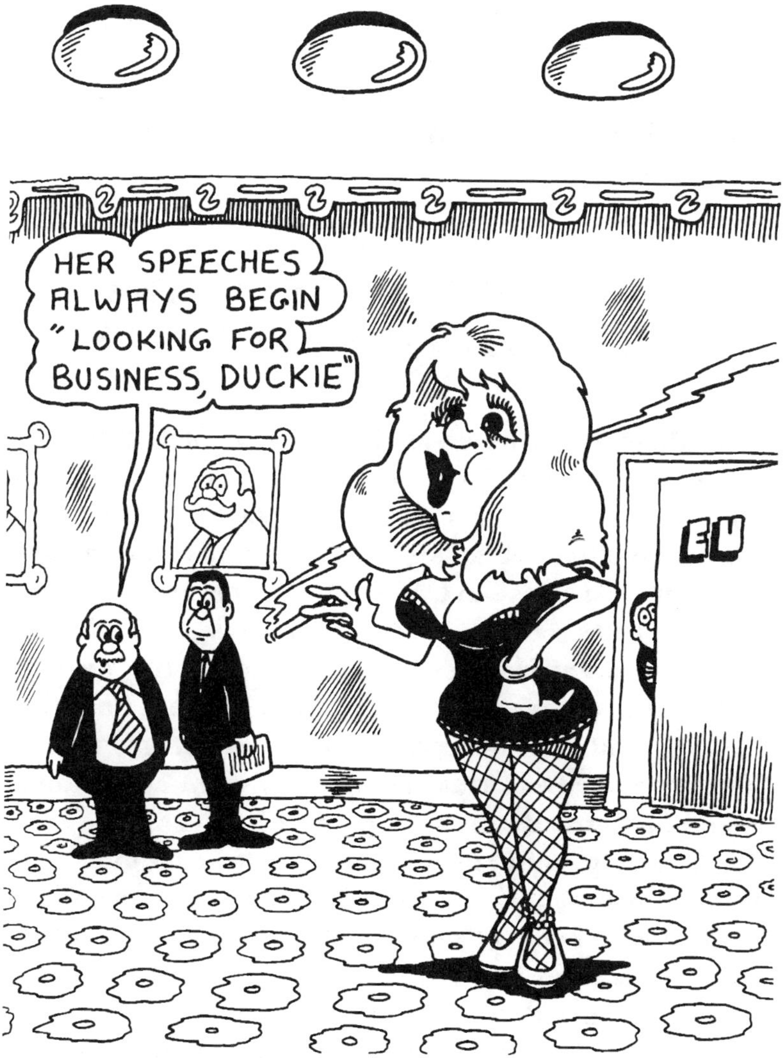

64

The second directive questions the legitimacy of the original manufacturer of our Caerphilly cheese. The question when is Caerphilly cheese not Caerphilly? When it is made in Caerphilly according to the Brussels bureaucrats. Mr Jenkin's small cottage industry is closed by Brussels bureaucracy because he gets unpasturised milk delivered in traditional metal milk churns. I say to hell with Brussels internal interference in our domestic life.

WASTED HIDDEN COSTS IN BRUSSELS BUREAUCRACY

Endless new directives flow into Whitehall for our civil service to act upon. Each directive costs Us Folk our hard earned cash to enact and satisfy the Brussels cloning machine. Road signs have all had to be changed to comply. Bridges have had to be strengthened.

New rules on packaging cosmetics and toiletries require a manufacturer to keep a data file on each product he manufactures with analysis of not only each product but its wrapping or packaging, with a laboratory analysis available at forty-eight hours notice should the bureaucrats wish to inspect it. This is costing our industry millions of pounds to comply. The problem is that they take an idea each time and follow through with their actions to the extreme. So much so, that, rather than reduce paperwork through a single market scheme they have tied industry up in a hotch potch of unnecessary bureaucratic knots that result in products costing us folk more at the point of sale. It's crazy, but typical when bureaucracy has a free hand.

All these and thousands of other directives come out of the national budgets or private industry building up

an enormous hidden cost that is particularly difficult to estimate. Commentators have put it at several hundred million a year but I think that could be just the tip of the iceberg.

BRITAIN'S TRADE WITH THE REST OF THE WORLD.

Britain's strength in the past has been its ability to produce products the world market required. Our industry has, in the eighties, undergone a radical change from an industrial base to a service led and specialist product industry. Despite this, our exporters have achieved a remarkable share of a growing technical market outside Europe, particularly in the middle and far East. Notable successes have been in markets that have previously been difficult to break into like Japan.

This happened because Britain has allowed foreign investment from Japan, Taiwan, Malaysia and other large investors who are looking for a manufacturing base in this area that is friendly. Two thirds of foreign investment in Britain comes from outside Europe. A similar percentage of Britain's foreign investments (60%) are outside Europe, returning around eighty-billion pounds a year. New markets are continually opening up in Asia, Latin America and the newly freed South Africa. All these countries need information technology, transport, Nuclear Power and indeed help in training their armies, police, down to public servants.

Trade with our traditional customers in the Commonwealth is on the increase. All this new trade is required to balance the deficit we run in trade within the EU.

Since our membership of the EU we have built a staggering trade deficit with Europe of one-hundred billion pounds and rising. So the promise that our future was bright inside a free trade Europe was another political con. Every moment we remain in this straight jacket it holds us back from realising the amazing success we are achieving elsewhere.

There is no reason why we can't trade with Europe but remain a free trade agent to sell our products to the best markets throughout the world. This follows our traditional instincts that held us in high esteem at the turn of the century.

Europe still takes fifty-three percent of our product, but this has fallen gradually over the last ten years. Soon our trade with the middle and far East will overtake our product sale to Europe. Why do our politicians, almost in unison, insist our future is unthinkable outside Europe?

Our heart is not and never has been in Europe. Seventy-two percent of the nation does not want to continue in a Europe of Jaques Delors impossible dream of a single currency leading to a single parliament.

Why don't our politicians insist the EU is turned round to what we first were told by the Rt. Hon. Edward Heath it was meant to be; A simple free trade area between European states with just an inspectorate to insure fair, unsubsidised trading and let competition do the rest. We do not need all this expensive cloning of industrial endeavour by the Brussels bureaucracy. Competition is by far the most effective and efficient leveller.

If this is not achieved we must get out of the EU straight jacket before it strangles us. What ever we do we must capitalise on our world trade success and divert energy from Europe to chase the winners. Our slogan should be; 'Europe under the peoples terms' or not at all.

CIVIL SERVANTS.

The mere combination of these two reasonably common words is emotive. A lifetime of dealing with them means that I could be classed as somewhat of an expert. If there is such a thing.

So what is a civil servant? A civil servant is quite simply a servant of the crown or to put it more accurately a servant of parliament. Isn't it strange that when you have dealt with them over many years you realise that this is absolute nonsense. You come to realise civil servants are a breed apart. They are the ruling class in deed if not in name.

They control, govern, devise and manipulate every aspect of our governed life and they are able to do so for one very simple reason. They are in their job for life.

Politicians, even ministers come and go, never really getting to grips with their latest promotion before they are moved up, sideways or down to their next appointment. This, above all else, is why civil servants can run rings around all of Us simple Folk.

The civil service is a vast octopus with its tentacles choking every facet of our lives. We cannot breathe, sleep, eat, holiday, drive, be ill, be old, or even die without interference from this monster. Yet it is meant to be an instrument of the people reflecting the politics of the incumbent government. It rules despite politicians and uses up nearly half our national gross product, (our gross national earnings) to do so. That is why we will never feel rich as long as this octopus wraps us up in its greedy, life draining grasp.

The top echelon of the civil service is the most exclusive club in Britain. Its members, who control the direction of the services from their high ranking offices,

form a band of elitism without parallel. Since they graduated from their universities, usually Oxford or Cambridge, they have risen to the height of power by ruthless determination and solid gold contacts. There they will stay because they are the faceless men. The brains behind the flow of political ideology that comes and goes.

More cynically speaking they outlast any minister through cunning and long service knowledge.

Decisions are made by this all powerful group in the sanctuary of their exclusive male only clubs in luxurious settings with all creature comforts surrounding them.

They truly believe they carry the god given power to decide our destiny from their enclaves of unreality and the painful fact is they probably do. Add to this that they firmly believe they are superior beings and you begin to see what the rest of us, including the politicians, are up against.

They are well schooled in the diplomatic art. They are so well entrenched, through years of experience handed down on retirement, that it is almost impossible to dislodge them from their seats of privilege. Even the most hardened politicians have given up in awe of the task.

It is from this solid base that these mandarins of the service thrive, insulated from the rigours of the real world outside and protected from failure by the manner of their job. Ostensibly carrying out the wish of parliament so no blunders, errors in judgement or complete foul ups are pinned on them. How easy life must be up there.

Now consider a typical enactment of government legislation and you will see how the minds of these mandarins work. They are for ever trying to get money out of our pockets. They are constantly aiming to increase the size and power of the civil service.

THE WALL

Well, this is really understating it slightly. It was more than just a wall. Perhaps I should go back to the beginning so you can understand the reason for what became a disaster.

It all began when a road improvement scheme directed a new major road through our area. We were told it would make a great difference to our local traffic but it never did. However that is another story.

A compulsory order was used to purchase the land and that included a strip belonging to our local park. No one really minded too much, as our park was big and we really could spare the small part that was to be used.

Our council changed the boundary fence to its new position and left them to get on with their road.

It took ages for anything to happen and I mean several years. Then the machinery moved in and started digging the place up. In its wake it damaged our park's border fence badly in several places and we started to complain, if the kids in the park were to get into the site area they could easily be injured.

Promises were made but nothing was done. The builders said it wasn't their responsibility and suggested we complain to the architect. The architect declined liability and suggested we complain to the department of the environment. This department wanted an official complaint and they would look into it. Some ten years later and after many reminders the looking glass at the DOE was wearing a tiny bit thin.

Well, the road was finally finished and opened by some junior minister. (Who, I seem to recall, was on a driving ban at the time.) Our fence now became a major hazard.

Our council wouldn't repair it as they said it was the clear duty of the DOE to accept liability. We could see a fatal accident occurring at any time. We realised a wall was now required to protect our children from the motorway so we got up a petition and eighty nine percent of the local residents signed it. Then at a local press conference we handed it to our MP. He seemed more interested in the clicking of cameras and making sure they spelt his name right than in the subject of our grievance. However he was our representative and this was the democratic way of handling the matter.

If at this moment we had felt relieved at the conclusion of our campaign it was ill founded. We had many months turning into years of work to complete before we saw the end. Yes, it had passed into the hands of the mighty army of civil servants at the DOE. A labyrinth of corridors each containing a multitude of offices, each office covering their own special brand of complications for reforms.

It was into this monster's hands this simple request for a safety wall at the end of our park found itself that day. After three months we enquired at the DOE for a progress report only to find out our paperwork had moved on to another department. This section in turn said they were studying it and would report as soon as they were finished. Every second month we would ring to be informed our paperwork had moved on. It seemed to be a monotonous game. It was so repetitive I counted eighteen moves in three and a bit years. Not bad for a simple wall, I thought.

It was almost at this time that the unthinkable happened. A young boy of nine followed his ball

through one of the not so small gaps in the fence and ran under a lorry. Needless to say he received fatal injuries.

As a tragedy often does, it concentrated minds and had the desired effect from the body politique. Especially our friend who likes to see his picture in print.

The debate ended in an agreement to build a wall. That was five years ago. I recall the MP claiming it as a victory for his hard campaigning for the wall. The truth is he did less than sod all, (Unless you count the photographs). He would tell you that this was publicity and that is what matters.

Now the civil service had to take notice. Parliament had passed the matter to them to enact.

I don't know about you but to me a simple almost straight wall, without gaps, doorways or frills is a straight forward job any builder, even with little experience, could undertake. Perhaps someone should tell that to the civil service. Maybe we should explain the word simple to the mandarins.

Remember, that is what we asked for in the first place.

Well, we didn't get it. Oh yes, we eventually got a wall, more suited to a football stadium than a back wall to a park. We were told the civil service knew best and had done exhaustive research to establish requirement and future use. A wall's a wall isn't it? Not, it seems, at this establishment.

After six months and no visible action, we ventured to enquire about progress towards completion only to be told the civil service was doing a feasibility study.

"But parliament gave the go ahead for a wall so what's the problem?"

"Well" I was told in a patronising manner, "we have to establish many facts before proceeding. For example the best position for the wall. "Surely where the fence is would do fine?" "We have to establish this by our tried methods. Then there is the question of height."

"Six to seven feet is the usual requirement to stop kids climbing over the wall." "We have to weigh this up against other criteria such as the position in relation to the road and of course the environmental appearance."

I never knew a simple wall had to have so much thought put into it." I said.

The civil serpent looked at me, venom pouring from his tongue. "We are paid to do the thinking." He said with condescension. Well, I never knew thinking was the sole prerogative of the civil service but there you go.

"Can you give me an idea when you will start building?"

"When we have finished our studies," came the curt reply. Like the hole in the bucket we had come full circle. No point in proceeding; I thought.

Six more months dragged by. Still no action. We had organised some of our elder citizens to help patrol the fence to try to prevent another accident but in the end analysis they were no match for the agile youth.

Nine months-then a year-still no action. I called at the DOE again. "Where is our wall?" I demanded with some forcefulness.

"Oh yes, your wall. We are getting on very well with that project. It is now undergoing a study for future use. Very satisfactory progress don't you think? Soon be in the hands of the architects."

"How soon?" I demanded.

"As soon as this report is finished."

You can't nail these guys down to time I realised. They don't know the meaning of time or urgency.

Procedure seems to replace time and requires civil servants to manage this dimension.

Suddenly it dawned on me. This was how in hundreds and thousands of similar simple acts the civil service mushroomed. First it took a simple idea, complicating it beyond recognition by passing it through this system. Man managing the whole scheme with civil servants. No wonder their ranks grew larger each year. What possible man-managing could they create from a simple wall?

"No. A wall doesn't need man management," I told myself, "does it?"

Well, it took a further two and a half years before we had the answer.

The environmental future survey was completed within a year. Then the wall went to the DOE's architect who delayed it another year. Half a year later the job was out to tender and we could at last pick up a plan of our wall. Well, simple it was not. Expensive it was. Our wall had turned into a fortress combining motorway toilet facilities, a security gate entrance for motorway users wishing to rest in the park picnic area, a fast food shop and of course a car park. This plan required some twenty four staff on shift to man it satisfactorily.

"There you are," said the civil serpent. "I told you we know best. Doesn't that plan show initiative?"

"But we only wanted a simple wall."

"You've got that and more with this design. Our boys certainly know their job."

"What's that," I said, "to complicate a simple matter and charge the bill to us folk? We only wanted a wall, not a meeting place for the rest of England's motorists."

It took them another two years to build their dream wall complex.

Our children will not use the park anymore as they don't enjoy the trouble they get from the motorway mob. So this simple wall ended up in destroying the very facility we wanted to protect, thanks, that is, to the civil serpents.

LANGUAGE AND THE PUBLIC

These extracts are from letters sent to government ministries. They were all written by members of the public, that's Us Folk.

1 I cannot get sick pay. I have six children. Can you tell me why this is?

2 This is my eighth child. What are you going to do about it? (How about sterilisation?)

3 My sister has no clothes and has not had any for years. The clergy have been visiting her. (We've all heard about clergy like that!!)

4 In reply to your letter, I have already cohabited with your officials so far without result. (So that is why the civil service keeps increasing!)

5 I am forwarding my marriage certificate, and two children, one of which is a mistake as you see.

6 I am glad to say that my husband, reported missing, is now dead. (Mrs Wentworth-Brewster?)

7 Unless I get my husband's money, I shall be forced to lead an immortal life.

8 I am writing these lines for Mrs G. who cannot herself write. She expects to be confined next week and can do with it. (We'll send our best man round!)

9 I am sending you my marriage certificate and six children. I had seven and one died, which was baptised on a half sheet of paper by the vicar.

10 Please find out if my husband is dead, as the man I am now living with won't eat or do anything until he is sure.

11 In answer to your letter, I have given birth to a little boy weighing eight pounds. Is this satisfactory?

12 You have changed my little girl into a little boy. Will this make a difference. (Wonderful what they can do these days at the ministry!)

13 Please send my money at once as I have fallen in errors with my landlord.

14 I have no children as my husband is a bus driver and works all day and night.

15 In accordance with your instructions, I have given birth to twins in the enclosed envelope. (Wasn't it a bit on the cramped side?)

16 I want money as quick as you can send it. I have been in bed with my doctor all week and he doesn't seem to be doing me any good. (I didn't know they supplied that on the national health service.)

17 Milk is wanted for my baby as the father is unable to supply it.

18 I am sorry my application is late but we have been very busy since my husband returned from seven months at sea.

19 I have a baby twelve months old. Thanking you for same, I am yours truly.

20 Please send me a form for the supply of milk for having babies at reduced prices.

21 I have a baby nine months old, fed entirely on cows and another child.

22 I have posted my form by mistake before my child was properly filled in.

23 Will you please send me a form for the supply of cheap milk? I have a baby two months old and didn't know it until a friend told me.

24 Sorry I have been so long in filling in the form, but I have been in bed two weeks with my baby and I didn't know it was running out till the milk told me.

25 Re your enquiry. The teeth at the top are all right. But the ones in my bottom are hurting terribly.

Each one a gem from Us Folks. You're all stars. Keep them rolling!

PARTY POLITICS

Party politics is like a boxing tournament;

THE BOXING MATCH

The party system supplies the contenders for the house of commons boxing ring.

In the blue corner we have the conservative party led by its present team captain the trotting Major. He is not quite on the same level as his predecessor, the Iron Lady, but trying hard to impress. They have the advantage of being in power for a whole decade without a knockout, just a change of team leader. I say an advantage, but after this sort of time they can't blame the ailments of the economy on anyone but themselves if they were to be honest.

Heck, when was the last time you heard of a politician being honest? They do try to blame the others and rely on Us Folk having a short memory. The trotting Major likes to think he is running a cricket team and always aims to give the impression he is playing with a straight bat. The house of commons is

OK, OK! PIGS FLY, THE EARTH IS FLAT AND NUCLEAR POWER IS SAFE..... BUT WHERE ON EARTH DID YOU GET THE "HONEST" AND "POLITICIAN" CONNECTION?
Edmunds

however a boxing ring and many a stray punch falls below the belt.

Major has his team of sparring partners who meet regularly to discuss tactics and arrange the fixtures list for the future tournaments. The whips perform the duty of the advertising agent, making sure all the seats are filled for important bouts.

Controlling the match from a vantage point the speaker oversees the in-fighting, cautioning the boxers who continually foul, and even stopping a contest if tempers start to fray.

It is the duty of the captain to make sure his team scores well so his senior team members all arrive prepared for a quick knockout, but this seldom occurs. The tournament has been known to go well into the night, especially when an opponent refuses to lie down.

At the end of the contest the side with the highest score wins. The whole process is controlled by the referee. Mr. Speaker.

In the red corner we had the fiery Welshman with his ready rhetoric born of the valleys. He had considerable trouble fielding a side that all pulled together. They had a nasty habit of fighting each other rather than their opponents in the blue corner. It has been known for them to boost their punching power by putting lead in their gloves.

Unfortunately for them the speaker has eagle eyes and dismisses them from the ring for cheating. Perhaps the largest disadvantage the red corner displays is its readiness by some of its team members to wear their colours in Day-Glow red. This blinds them to the reality of their fight and leaves the blue corner as outright champions for fifteen years in a row. Try as he would he could not get his team to pull together. If he had managed he could have mounted a challenge but as Harold Wilson was overheard to say to one of his golfing

partners; 'I do not lead a single party but a multi-party federation. I spend my life balancing on a rope of decision and pray I don't fall off.' Things haven't changed much, have they? To his credit he has dismissed some trots but as soon as he sacks one batch another group turns up to haunt him, spoiling his team unity. A divided team will never rule. He was replaced by a Smith who sadly died and was replaced by an ultra conservative type called, affectionately, Bambi. Now he could bring the blue corner down by adopting their training schedule, thus voiding their performance.

So why the long winning streak for the blue corner? Maybe the reason is simply because Us Folk can't stomach extremes of any colour governing us. It is only fair to mention there are in existence some twenty odd free lance boxers loosely linked to two or three other minor clubs with the exception of one useful heavy weight. In the main their performance is poor so their only chance will come when there is a stalemate situation. Still they wait in hope.

So that is party politics contribution to the house of commons yearly knockout event, I think we should ban boxing; don't you?

THE POLITICAL PIRANHA.

For over two decades Northern Ireland has been an insoluble problem for our Parliamentarians. We have seen the Baader-Meinhof gang from Germany and the Red Army faction from Italy come and go, defeated by tough government action but the IRA and the UVF problem remains to haunt us like a Piranha in a sea of endless time. Peace talks, we've seen it all before: the

86

latest round of talks is more to impress the American electorate than to broker peace in Ireland. If the IRA honestly want peace they would hand in their illegal arms.

In just over two decades nearly three thousand innocent people have lost their lives. Thousands more have been seriously injured. Billions of pounds worth of property has been destroyed and a large part of our army is deployed in an effort to police this hopeless impasse.

We have even seen a series of bombs in Dublin, over the border, involving simultaneous explosions, killing thirty-three people and maiming many others, carried out by the UVF with cowardly, unspecified help.

Attacks have been made on animals, the horse guards, shoppers at Harrods, pubs in towns on the mainland and in Northern Ireland and buildings in the City of London. All these attacks caused death and destruction.

So who are these Humans, justifying their cowardly attacks on our state by using sentiments from the past that are no longer relevant, that hold people subservient to their demands?

They are a handful of very rich men who have made their fortune out of subversion and aim to continue to do so by selective terrorism and perpetuating a religious divide through propaganda. They use their skills in public relations far better than the fumbling state system and lose no opportunity to discredit even well-meaning actions by the state. They even seem to be able to turn murderous terrorists into heroes while in jail for their crimes against the people. That's Us Folk. The press perpetuate this folly.

We have waited patiently while our politicians have fumbled their way from one disaster to another. Even when people have been gaoled for heinous crimes against Us Folk, we find on appeal the convictions have not been safe. Our authorities seem to have taken short roots to convictions, giving the IRA once more ample propaganda on a plate. We have also witnessed the European courts give compensation to a convicted terrorist for twisting her ankle. Compensation twice as great as that given to a victim of her speciality in crime. It is nothing short of a gross scandal and an insult to the relatives of the innocent victims.

So is it the insoluble problem of the century or are our politicians just incapable of biting the bullet?

If they continue with the stale policies that have been proved useless against terrorism the problem is here to stay. Until they can accept that terrorism cannot be beaten by conventional, democratic methods, there is no hope of success.

No state can adequately guard against terrorist attacks.

The terrorist chooses targets, hits and withdraws without logic or obvious reason. They do so for maximum publicity.

We have literally thousands of such targets that could suit their aim.

The IRA structure is such that it is designed to stop infiltration reaching its inner sanctum, employing a cell system with few trusted, long serving, sympathisers linking cells to the top council.

The IRA is however, small in numbers and the top council of rich receivers can be counted quickly. Through dedicated work, these men and their movements are known to our security service. The top council are in their tens. The active terrorists are in their hundreds but their source of revenue is in the thousands, many of which are reluctant contributors or paying to a fund to protect their job. The IRA has replaced its funding from supporters, as they dwindled, to favour a network of local extortions in Ireland and the mainland. For example, the IRA and the UVF run protection rackets covering most taxi drivers in Belfast. No taxi driver can safely operate without paying part of his earnings to one fund or the other and in many cases both.

Certain pubs in Irish areas of London, such as Kilburn have regular collections for IRA funds. If you don't pay up you won't be served and if you cause trouble you are likely to be attacked and even knee-capped. Everything they do they do by fear.

Irish workers in the building trade in this country when they work for certain large Irish owned companies in the demolition business, have to pay into a special fund. They will find they are out of a job if they refuse; so they mostly comply. Protection rackets are by no means the sole source or even the largest supply of funds.

It is well known how the misguided Irish emigrants in America belonging to Noraid collect funds that go towards buying arms for the IRA's terrorist pursuits.

It does not stop there. A cell in Malmo, Sweden trades in drugs in the Amsterdam open market and on the European drug markets bringing millions to the IRA cause. In other areas the IRA traders deal in arms not only for their own use but act as arms agents for the subversive elements in the world bringing millions more to the IRA fat cat funds.

The IRA are the best organised fund raisers in terrorist circles. The UVF have tried in a less professional way to follow their example.

However the funds are mostly obtained through illegal practices and, therefore, represent a potential point of weakness from which to attack their organisation. The government, having failed to stem their fund raising, are shown to be impotent.

When you add up the millions made by the IRA fund-raising effort it becomes clear that they do not spend anything like the figure raised to run their terrorist activities. To them it is a question of skimming the top of the fund for publicity to perpetuate the flow of money. It is in the end analysis a huge business in the hands of the chosen few.

So how can we stop the company trading? It is relatively simple compared to the failed political and military initiatives so far used. It does, however, need a certain type of political leader who is prepared to say 'enough is enough' and use the tactics Churchill insisted were the only way to beat Hitler and that is to meet them head on at their own level.

If we were to announce that we would kill a top IRA council member for every death caused by their bombing campaigns or planned assassinations and we proved our dedication by so doing, the IRA's ruthless policy would soon come to a halt.

We have the knowledge within our security services and we have the expertise within our SAS. Have we got the guts within our leadership? It is a war, so the IRA command is a legitimate target. This policy should be applied equally to the IRA and UVF and include Southern Ireland and the mainland as legitimate areas of operation. Very soon the top council of the IRA would cave in or be eliminated. Both ways the firm would be out of business.

Lets make sure there is another failed company soon, or will our politicians wait until another three thousand innocent people die?

PUBLIC SERVICES

There are a number of public services managed by the State, Local authorities and indeed private enterprise. I can only cover two now and one later of the most important areas:

HEALTH

Health effects us all. It is therefore the most emotive service run by government and has always remained as one of the top priorities for politicians. The idea of a National Health Service was the brain-child of a remarkable man, Lord Beveridge, a member of the Liberal party and a man with a great knowledge of reform. The simple conception, a free health service for all, is to this day the bed rock of our health care system.

The certainty remains that no government dare dismantle or even dismember the service for fear of being savaged at the polls. Nevertheless the service by the mid seventies was becoming an ever increasing financial burden on the state. Costs were escalating and new techniques were bringing cures to patients previously regarded as incurable. Heart surgery was taking massive strides forward, as was hip replacement. It was cures like these that revolutionised health care but also brought their own problems. Long waiting lists for operations and accusations of health care mis-management levelled at the government. None of these were helped by the escalating cost of a top heavy non productive administration.

The eighties have caused the necessity for a total rethink about the aims and objectives of the health service. This has created much doubt and anxiety in the minds of Us Folk as to the intentions of our political masters. It is reassuring to know no government can touch the service without a massive outcry within the nation but we must allow the service to move with the times. The new reforms have brought with them, in their wake, an unacceptable layer of management which in turn is wasting precious resource that could be used on care.

Finance must never be allowed to take away a patient's right to emergency treatment. This uncaring city slicker attitude must be outlawed. Emergency takes preference over all.

Certainly an effort has been made to bring the service out of the doldrums of the seventies. The result will not be known for several years to come although early figures are encouraging. It is painfully plain that without this effort our health service would have collapsed. So we must be vigilant but patient. A healthier service is worth the wait. When we cease to wait for surgery our service will be restored. Those that are waiting in pain especially long for this day.

The first person that you see when you are ill is your doctor. He is a diagnostic post box for your complaint. It is down to him to evaluate your ailment and let it cure itself, with maybe mild medicine to assist, or send you to a specialist for examination. Nature cures most of our ailments better than we understand, and your doctor relies on this when deciding which course to take.

Behind your local practitioner is a host of specialists some are surgeons able to diagnose and repair your body ailments. These range from heart specialists to gynaecologists, eye specialists to anal experts.

They are backed by hospital staff capable of nursing you, x-raying you and preparing you for surgery in extreme cases. Then there are the emergency teams at hand to deal with accident and emergency cases. The dedicated ambulance crews that actually fight sometimes to get you to hospital. The nurses and doctors that access you and prepare you for surgery or medical attention, and the surgeons that repair you. Finally the nurses that help you back to health after your operation. It is difficult to appreciate them till you have been in their hands. It is then almost impossible not to attribute to them your recovery.

Behind this army of dedicated medical practitioners are the research teams that analyse our samples and give data to our doctors to reinforce their diagnosis. There are teams dedicated to so far incurable diseases such as cancer, and the latest, most terrifying disease to hit mankind, Aids.

Then there are the pharmaceutical companies all developing their own brands of cures and pain killers to assist us in our illness. It is an immense caring industry that sometimes, not too often, gets things wrong. They are human, like us, after all.

The service is even now, over managed with top heavy administration. It must be hoped this is under constant review and every effort is being made to lighten this burden that is a major contributor to its escalating costs.

Junior doctors do much of the medical work within the hospital services. Their working hours and condition of service would not be accepted by Us Folk. Their case needs urgent review.

I, for one say a big "thank you" to all our caring people in this great service.

WHOOPS, THAT'S THE WRONG BIT

The letter that dropped through my door that morning brought me instant mental relief from my long suffering. It was as if I had been in pain for eight months awaiting my turn for surgery. The intermittent agony had worn me down and not knowing when help would come made it worse. At least now I could see light at the end of the tunnel. The letter contained a date when my suffering, with luck, should end. I was due to sign in for my operation in ten days time. I can't say I was looking forward to the event but the date represented a release from my physical condition and offered a reprieve from my prison.

On the appointed day I arrived at the hospital having followed instructions and had nothing to eat or drink at breakfast.

After the usual signing in ceremony I was taken by a nurse to the ward and allocated a bed for my stay. Being the last bed in the row I had only a bed to my left in which an elderly gentleman seemed to be fast asleep. The noise emanating from his person resembled a local pig farm I once visited.

Having drawn the curtain I changed into my pyjamas and made myself comfortable in the rather hard bed while I awaited the consultant that was due to examine me before my operation.

I soon tired of the traction engine next to me. I decided to escape the repetitive monotony by placing the headphones over my ears, not so much to listen to the music on the radio as to escape his dreadful chorus.

The hospital was old in its structure, having large windows by each bed and high ceilings in need of fresh paint. It smelt generally of cleaners and surgical spirit.

The nurses were bustling around attending to the patients' needs, and administrating the medicine to each individual prescription. Matron, a grey haired portly woman in her mid fifties, was directing the operation with the precision and command of a regimental sergeant major.

Suddenly the ward went quiet. The double doors burst open and a distinguished looking man in his late forties briskly walked into the ward. He was followed by a motley bunch of young, white coated, housemen badly in need of expert help with their attire.

Matron greeted him formally and proceeded to conduct his tour from bed to bed. At each stage he was given full details of each patient before he examined them, and proceeded to discuss each case with his band of housemen.

Seeing him assert his authority and knowledge in such a manner while trying to share his expertise with a less than attentive band of students left me confident to surrender to his obvious ability. So when it came to my turn his credentials were impeccable in my mind and confidence in his skill was absolute. His final diagnosis confirmed my doctor's finding and if possible, increased my trust.

The result of my medical diagnosis was that my Gall Stone was such a whopper that it had denied all medical remedies to disintegrate it. They would have to operate to remove my Gall Bladder to relieve my discomfort. This all seemed logical so I accepted it without question.

The operation was set for three o'clock that afternoon and I settled down to rest before my big event as best I could with the traction engine in full roar next

to me. I eventually had to beg cotton wool from the nurse to ensure I got some peace.

My big moment had at last arrived. I was woken by a young nurse who refused me even a cup of tea in case it should make me throw up while I was under anaesthetic. I was dressed in an operation gown and the second nurse came with a razor. I innocently thought she was going to shave me for my big moment. She did but not in the usual place.

After that episode I threw modesty out of the window! It wasn't long before the ward sister came with a strange look of resolution on her face and announced; "Come on now, it's time for your pre-med." Thinking this was a pre-operation examination I proclaimed; "Come on then I'm all yours." On reflection not the best of remarks.

With the ease of a wrestler she turned me over, pulled up my operation gown and produced the largest needle on the end of a tube I have ever seen.

"This won't hurt," she said and plunged the needle deep into my buttock. It did. The entry of the needle produced an instant reflex of my buttock muscles and I felt the ripping of the muscle fibre. Then came the expansion of the area as the fluid entered till the fibres seemed to burst. It left a vicious pain not unlike cramp.

In the next few minutes I was in too much agony to consider whether the injection was taking effect by making me relaxed and drowsy or not.

As the pain partly subsided I considered my state and I concluded I was becoming hyperactive. The nurse brushed it off by saying I would soon become relaxed and drowsy. I didn't. I started a tour of the ward, trying to liven up what seemed to be a room full of drowsy people.

The nurse, so concerned, called an orderly to physically subdue me and return me to my bed.

It seemed ages before I was taken, on a trolley, to the anaesthetist's waiting clutches.

"Now I am going to give you a small jab and by the time you have counted ten you will be away."

I felt a pressure on my arm but nothing to produce the pain the sister had inflicted on me. It is an amazing fact how much of your life flashes bye at a time like this. I seemed to relive my precious memories as I counted; Five,....Six,....Seve..... I was spiralling up as if lifted by a whirlwind, into a land of complete comfort and joy.

I distinctly remember being very annoyed at awakening, as if it had been so much more enjoyable in the other land of my mind; a paradise disturbed. A nurse seemed to be leaning over me and concertinaed in and out of focus. My vision resembled that of a fish. I seemed to look up a long, dark tube at a ray of light with the nurse's head in central focus. A voice, which seemed detached from my vision's picture said; "He's coming round now, everything will be all right." My mouth was dry and in a voice I didn't recognise I asked for a scotch on the rocks.

Another voice from somewhere outside my vision but undoubtedly familiar exclaimed; "That's typical. He must be all right." I fell back into a deep sleep maybe to escape these paradise breakers. I was eventually awakened by the consultant's entourage discussing the finer points about the man in the next bed, and after exhausting their dialogue about his ailments they moved towards me.

The consultant, in his best bedside manner, bent over me and asked; "How are we now it's all over?" "Fine." I said, "A bit sore but I suppose it will pass." "Let's take a look." Said the consultant as he uncovered my stomach. His expression turned to one of shock. "They've removed the wrong bit. This was a gall bladder operation. They've taken out his appendix."

By this time the consultant was racing to the swing doors followed by matron in hot pursuit.

The students stood, some aghast, some in hysterics, not knowing whether to follow or remain. Sister came to the rescue when she saw my discomfort and removed them from sight.

Needless to say I had a second dose of paradise followed by a rude awakening, but this time they removed the right bit.

I am so very thankful that the operation that was confused with mine did not feature the removal of an arm, leg or something VITAL!!

SURGEONS CONFERENCE

After the Micro surgeons conference in New York, the leading surgeons were in the bar and, being drunk as skunks began to reminisce over their greatest feats.

The first, an Australian surgeon explained: "We had a chap caught in a printing press at a factory last year and all that was left of him was his little finger. Our team of surgeons constructed a new hand and built a new arm, engineered a new body and ultimately, when he returned to the workforce, he was so efficient he put five men out of work."

"That's nothing", said the American surgeon. "We had a worker trapped inside a nuclear reactor and all that was left of him was his hair. We constructed a new skull, a new torso and new limbs, then returned him to the work force. He is so efficient, he has now put fifty men out of work.

The English surgeon was not to be outdone!

99

"I was walking down the street when I came upon the smell of a fart, so I took it back to the hospital in a garbage bag, let it loose on the operating table and we got to work. First of all we wrapped an anus around it, built a bum around that, attached a body to one end and legs to the other. Gradually it turned into a politician, who became chancellor of the exchequer, and he put the whole bloody country out of work. (No prize for guessing who!!)

EDUCATION

A pre-requisite to education, and an essential part of it, is literacy and numeracy. They are both required for advancement in education and coping with modern living requirements.

Just imagine driving without being able to read the road signs or shopping without the ability to add up what you have bought, then you will see how basic these two skills have become.

Education is essential to the development and for the future of any country. Badly handled it can turn a prosperous nation into a third rate also ran. It can also have the reverse effect if handled with skill. There are however, other important factors that complicate the formula, for instance the wealth of the nation necessary to afford good education. Then there is the quality and dedication of the teachers, and administrators to follow the right programme for education. It also depends on the willingness of the pupils to commit themselves to being educated, but most of all the parents commitment to seeing that their children improve their chance in life, particularly in the hard, struggle in todays world.

The parents, above all other influences, hold the future of their children in their grasp. The state, however hard it tries, cannot control the influence set by the parents. Far more attention should be paid to parent power and its effects.

Educationalists today use statistics as much as economists use figures to prove their point. If you get five economists in a room they will all vie with each other to prove their own blinkered pet theory.

This is the case with the majority of Educationalists. Progressive education has gained ground since the mid-seventies but it is only now that this system has shown up its main flaw. A high percentage of teenagers who can't read and write properly and are unable to add up. This perpetuates itself through the system ending up with school leavers that cannot cope in the hard world of realism that awaits them and ultimately leaves the country at a disadvantage.

So where has it all gone wrong? It is not bad planning that has caused this chasm in our education, but rather too much planning backing the wrong horse.

It has been obvious to Us simple Folk for some time that education had taken the wrong turning. There are five main elements that have to gel to create the right atmosphere for learning:

The programme or syllabus. The school. The teachers. The pupils and the parents.

PROGRAMME

To my way of thinking the most important step we could take to insure literacy and numeracy is to introduce pre-school education for three to five year olds. This will enable them to learn the basic framework of reading, writing and addition before their formal schooling.

If politicians really wish to solve the literacy problem they can by introducing this addition to schooling. This is a period of great intake potential in a child's development. A child with pre-school education behind them would find their future learning ability greatly enhanced. This addition, together with a traditional reading and writing programme and a basic numeracy introduction, will be the greatest step forward in education this century, because everything follows on from this point.

THE SCHOOL

The second largest problem in education today is the difference between schools, largely created by their area and social mix. This is the most difficult problem to overcome as socially deprived areas that need the best teachers seldom get them.

If you consider education from an unbiased view several interesting facts emerge.

The first is that private schools or state schools do not have a monopoly on good education, neither do they have better learning facilities. There are good and bad schools in both sections.

There were three factors that I studied when choosing a school for my children. First, I considered the quality of the head teacher. Second, the manner in which they managed the arts department, a very telling factor in the development of any child's character.

Third, I closely examined the out of class activities available to the children to broaden their interests. Activities like drama and public speaking are every bit as important to some students as formal education. A broad mix of activities means a school is trying to cater for all the needs of their pupils.

Children, above all else, need stimulation. A school that achieves this will certainly succeed. Another interesting statistic is that schools under the state system generally have better facilities for the sciences than private schools. Their laboratories and libraries are usually better equipped, but in the end analysis it is the quality of the teachers that really makes the difference. They must be able to stimulate their pupils to enable them to discover their subject.

Something that really bothers me is the new practice of publishing school performance tables. It is dangerous and wrong. I would personally stop this new desire on behalf of the media to publish results of our schools and form them into a league table for a very important reason. It encourages schools to only put their brightest pupils forward for exams where they know they will get good results. This would effectively leave the less able students in a state of educational limbo.

THE TEACHERS

We have all heard our children say; "That was a really interesting lesson in History", or, "That Math's teacher is boring." When you get this form of feed back it is easy to assess that your child will do much better in history than in maths. Teaching is a skill but its winning edge comes from the vocational quality of the

teacher. Any intelligent person can learn a method of teaching, but far fewer can captivate a classroom full of gigglers and keep their interest for thirty to forty-five minutes. Yet it is such teachers that get the best results.

It was on precisely this point that the Plowden report failed to grasp the consequences of their findings. They had seen good results from pilot schemes, run by specially trained and motivated teachers, using the then new idea of progressive teaching. What they failed to realise with all their knowledge and academic superiority was that when the progressive teaching was introduced as mainstream thinking within education the specialist teachers would be replaced by the good, bad and the indifferent teachers within the profession. So good teachers are an essential ingredient for high performing schools.

Another reason that league tables should not be published is that some schools, due to their location, struggle to get results. That doesn't mean that they don't try very hard but that the cards are stacked against them. Bad parent attitude, drug usage and truancy are daily problems for teachers; distracting them from their real job, teaching.

These are the problems in too many schools today. The educators must work hard to eradicate them. The quality of teaching is also important if we want to raise the standards within the problem schools and eliminate the teacher factor as a source of bad results. Too many Educationalists have been drawn away from traditional teaching methods with little thought to the end result. They seem more interested in experimenting with our future, the youth. This simple story shows the power of our tradition expressed through our literary past.

PROSPECTIVE

Recently, only last week in fact, I read the result of a survey. You know the kind of thing: eighteen months of research at a cost of several hundred thousand pounds to discover something which any granddad, granny, mother, father, man or woman in the supermarket has accepted as a fact of life. The survey I'm talking about discovered that children that dodge school do not have as good an education as those that don't.

Before you giggle or throw up your hands in despair, let us examine the credentials of the people who were commissioned, at great expense, to conduct the survey. A probation officer, a child psychiatrist, a prison officer, a single mother plucked from a council estate and three members of parliament. My information is that they held a meeting at which the probation officer sat quietly, the psychiatrist became confused, the prison officer nodded and the three MP's carried their proposal to visit the West Indies in order to study black children's behavioural patterns.

After three weeks of intense enquiries on the sun-kissed beaches of Jamaica, the dear heroes of parliament flew home with their sun-tans and souvenirs, convened a meeting, told everybody what they already knew, bullied their co-committee members into acquiescence and issued a statement about kids being better off in school than out. I'm glad the politicians had their way. For me it was another example of the politician's self gratification when the baby kissing is no longer necessary.

I'm on to surveys so I'll mention another. Cheaper this time: only one hundred and seventy-five thousand quid of taxpayers money, provided reluctantly most of the time and at all times spent without reference to wallet or purse holder. The result of this survey, which is supposed to shudder us to the point where our socks blow off, announces that: 'People that study the science are superior to people who study the arts.'

I'm not qualified to pass judgements or even comments on scientists. I still tie my shoe-laces with my fingers. I open my curtains without the assistance of gadgetry and my cooker I light with a match. It's all very simple, this every day life of mine, separated from micro-chips and micro-things and what have you and I haven't yet found the need for a computer which automatically makes early morning tea. Simple soul, that's me. However, my dander can be raised and raised it is by so called analysts who claim that the bunsen-burner is superior to the book.

A while back I went to a dinner party. The host worked somewhere surrounded by test tubes. His wife wrote poetry and cooked a very good meal. The last dish eaten, the coffee served and half drunk, Mary stood up and reached out for dirty dishes.

"I'd better clear the table," she said, gathering plates. Peter, her husband of ten years, didn't glance up or pause for breath, instead he continued to talk about something which threatened to put me to sleep half an hour earlier.

"I'll give you a hand," I said.

"So will I," the girl in the flowered dress said.

"Me too," chorused her boyfriend and two other guests.

In the kitchen Mary washed, I rinsed, Jo dried, Susan stacked and Bob and Shirley wiped the tops. When we had finished Mary made fresh coffee,

produced a bottle of cheap brandy, spiked our drinks and smiled a lot.

For two hours the six of us engaged in conversation. We discussed topics as diverse as Shakespeare and Morecambe and Wise. We laughed at memories of Tommy Hanley and in an instant, opinioned on Chaucer, Charles Lamb, Boswell, Samuel Johnson, Coleridge and Wordsworth. There were differences, but mainly we were joined by a common factor: emotion, something that literature can provide and science cannot.

As we gathered our coats and bid our thanks, I held Mary's hand a little longer than was necessary.

"You know," I said, "these guys can send a man to the moon and bring him back. I think that is incredible."

Mary smiled in that wonderful way nice people have.

"It's not that incredible," she said softly, turning her head to look at the sky and then staring into my eyes, "no, going there isn't incredible. What is incredible is the moon to which man can go."

No matter how hard I tried the car wouldn't start. Peter took off his coat, lifted the bonnet and fiddled around.

"Give it a try," he said.

I pushed the button and the engine fired. Peter wiped his hands and in the half light of the doorway I saw Mary shrug her shoulders.

Maybe, after all, the scientist and the poet can, well, whatever they can.

THE STUDENTS

All children have their own speed and capability for learning. A good teacher will access and then use their absorbing ability to the maximum.

Nearly all children have a thirst for knowledge. Ask any mother about the constant bombardment of questions that can drive her crazy. A good teacher will harness this to a sound learning pattern and channel the energy fruitfully.

A child is borne without knowledge or prejudice, while the years go by a child will develop its knowledge from its parent's influence. Later the child develops from influences at school, so that early development can effect the whole life of that child.

It is vitally important, as I have already said, to get children off to a good start with informal teaching between three and five years old. The importance of this cannot be stressed enough.

A child is malleable, first by the parents and after that by the teachers. If the parents fail badly only the best teachers can hope to influence the learning pattern. This is why problem areas need the best teachers.

PARENTS

Parents have the greatest influence on their child's life. It is this influence that can develop a child's future even before it starts formal education.

A happy secure family gives confidence to a child and this successfully clears the first major hurdle towards a good education. A feuding family gives even a bright child a distinct disadvantage. So time devoted within education to develop care through the parent teacher associations is time well spent. These associations are best placed to get other parents involved. A good school will encompass all parents and encourage them to take part in the school's activities. This co-operation bears much fruit.

Schools where parents won't co-operate are doomed to a second rate education regardless of the teacher's ability. These schools have a large number of parents that didn't want their children in the first place. In extreme cases they treat them to all sorts of abuse, or in some cases are just unable to cope with children. On the other end you have parents that are forced, through circumstance, to send their children to these schools, fearing that they will suffer through association. Unfortunately in this area education can only hope for change by evolution.

Parents are the king pin to education, so we should change our ways to improve our children's future: It's worth it Folks.

PLOWDEN'S PIRANHA

The Plowden report was a disaster for our children. Well, I know that now. They say you always have to do everything twice to get it right. I hope they don't do a second Plowden report. One was quite enough.

It all started in the early seventies for me. Suddenly I was widowed, which came as a thunderbolt out of the blue.

My husband had been a good provider and managed all our affairs without bothering me with their details.

Suddenly I was plunged into the job without notice and had an acute problem with our son, who had taken his father's death very badly. He had become withdrawn and moody and try as I would, I could not change his temperament.

Added to this I could no longer afford the private school he had been attending as a day boy so I was forced to consider one of three local schools in the state system.

I didn't know too much about schools. I discussed it with friends and the new school at the other end of town seemed to have the modern approach to education that interested me. So after discussing it with the headmaster, who seemed to know his job, I decided this was the school for Mark.

It seemed this new progressive education might just solve his moods and allow him to find his own level. It all fitted nicely to his needs. Well, I thought it did. At first it all seemed to be going well. Mark, who was just eight, seemed to be settling in well and as the weeks went by he seemed to be coming out of his retreat and behaving almost normally again.

This naturally pleased me but it also blinded me to what was happening to his character. There is nothing like success to blind you to the dangers. He was gradually becoming arrogant, off hand and idle. This was totally unlike the old Mark who was an energetic, good natured young man. Well, it took me six months to realise what had happened and a lot longer to find the source of the trouble.

You see you never suspect the school when it appears to have initially succeeded, so I tried in vain to find a reason outside school for his behavioural problem. One day, just by chance, I found myself up a ladder trying to fix a new light and to save coming down I asked Mark to read the instructions to me. To my

112

utter horror he couldn't read properly. He stumbled and stuttered over quite simple words. Now he was nearly nine years old and other kids of his age could read, write and add successfully. I knew that there was something seriously wrong.

I wasn't totally convinced by the headmasters assessment when he excused his bad reading by saying he was still suffering from the death of his father. However as he used plausible arguments to back his conjecture I accepted and bowed to his superior knowledge.

Over the next six months the situation did not change. By the time of his first report I knew I must take a serious decision. Most of the teachers gave standard non committal statements about Mark. One teacher's remarks stood out along side the others. This was his history teacher.

He said; "Mark's ability to comprehend this subject is severely impaired by his lack of reading and writing skill.

Furthermore he requires discipline to master these skills not available from progressive teaching."

I am eternally grateful to this teacher, as he woke me from the trance I had suffered since being brainwashed by his headmaster.

I knew he must go back to his old school. Not because it was fee paying but because they knew where they left off. To my surprise with a covenant and assisted place I could reduce the fees by two thirds and just about manage the cost. After six months he was back on course and reading well. I hope by relating this story it will make Educationalists think twice before changing tried and tested systems for whims in their privileged imagination. I also hope it will stop politicians creating change for change's sake.

To the Plowden committee; I wish them retirement.

RELIGION

Far down inside most of us is a deep rooted belief in some form of Religion. This may not be linked to any formal group, indeed it may just be a desire to help our fellow men while on earth. This aspiration happens to be a part of the itinerary of the Humanitarian Society.

It is this deep rooted sense that guides our lives and controls our behaviour. It has developed through the events that preceded us. Passed on by our forebears and developed by the agenda that influences the direction of our life.

Man, to help guide his belief, has made temples to the Gods to channel his emotional desire to belong, into his chosen church of worship.

Unfortunately from these man made Religions we are labelled a Protestant, Roman Catholic, Jew, Muslim, Hindu or one of a hundred other sects. Arising from this terrible labelling man has created barriers around our simple wishes to believe and belong.

Crusades of murder have been used by Religion since man took up arms, and is still being used by leaders like Saddam Hussein and the lieutenants of the IRA. On close analysis these claims of a justified battle in the name of some Religion or other are false and they always have been. They have been heisted upon Us poor and simple Folk using Religion to hide the real reason for the fight. Power as in Saddam's case or financial gain from the everlasting promotion of terrorism and murder in Northern Ireland, so it is that man uses his secular disguise for personal or image improvement.

No man of true religious conviction could, or would, condone the atrocities of either these examples. Yet going back in history most of the major Religions have been involved in such crusades of cruelty.

To hold a position of power and influence, the churches have had to create a wealth to give a base for their standing.

This wealth, particularly in the case of the Roman Catholic Church, has come from Us poor and simple Folk, collected gradually each day of prayer and invested over the ages un-taxed. At this present time the Roman Catholic Church has become the largest real estate owner in the world. Directly in contrast to their teaching that the earth belongs to us all.

THE OFFERTORY

When finance is mentioned, I always think about the story of the three heads of church who found themselves travelling in a railway compartment together. At first they hid themselves behind their papers and indulged themselves in a typical British Rail traveller's pose. The time eventually came when they had all finished their papers. After looking around at each other and out of the window the vicar from the church of England put a question to the other two;

"Gentlemen, it is indeed a rare opportunity to find a representative of each of the three main Religions travelling together. I have always been curious to know how the other Religions handle the offertory collected every service. On my part, in our church, we have a charity of the week and it goes to that charity. That is except Easter Sunday when it is blessed and taken as a gift from the parishioners to the vicar."

"We have a similar system," the Roman Catholic priest declared, "a collection is made each week and seventy five percent goes to the charity of the week and twenty five percent towards the upkeep of the church."

The Rabbi, sitting in the corner, rubbed his hands together and said;

"Boys, We have got a much better system. We take the collection on the golden salver and proceed to the high altar. We look up to heaven and say to god; Take what you want. We then throw the offering into the air, he takes what he wants and the rest comes back to us."

Perhaps that is why you never hear of a destitute Rabbi.

Religions have had their problems as well when it comes to money.

While the Roman Catholic church pleads poverty it is for ever holding out a begging hand. It has not only accumulated real estate making it the richest and largest landowner in the world today, but it also has a wealth of silver, gold and art treasures. This is true even in the third world countries where it is paid for by peasant pittances.

The church's investment in industry has undergone a change. The last Pope decided to clean up the church's public image concerning its wealth and accordingly ordered a large programme of dis-investment. The idea was to remove investment from the doors of the Vatican and hide it behind the walls of the Swiss banking system.

Unfortunately he chose as his financial adviser a dishonest banker called Sindona. Sindona used the sales of the church investments to launder drug money from the Mafia, and to operate all sorts of skims and scams. The church to this day claims it did not lose money. Therefore they must have a mountain of dirty money in their coffers. Which only goes to prove that where money is concerned morals quickly go out of the window.

During this period it was found that the Roman Catholic church owned a pharmaceutical company in Italy that had contraceptive pills as one of their products. Nothing like joining the devil to skim him!

Politics is a subject that politicians think the church should leave alone, concentrating solely on the spiritual side as their domain. In the world today is this possible?

A priest or bishop develops their dialogue through the problems that confront them daily.

Therefore it is not unreasonable that the bishop of Liverpool is moved by the abject poverty and hopelessness seen in Liverpool and sides with the peoples feeling of complete despair. By siding with this worthy cause he is promptly labelled a left wing Bishop, neutralising any good he can do.

He is also seen as belonging to the very group of left wing loonies that helped to accelerate the spread of poverty. So how do heads of Religion voice a view of reason? In many cases it's a "catch twenty-two" situation I suspect and therefore best assaulted as theory outside an ongoing situation. By doing it this way you remove the threat to political endeavour but you lose impact. Probably a worthwhile compromise.

I believe man-made Religions are merely a convenient focus point for our inability to comprehend the unanswered questions of our universe. Therefore it is man made religions that influence our willingness to comprehend by masking us from the truth.

118

An American research team reported that the head of the Roman Catholic Church in America back in February '54, stopped President Eisenhower from disclosing details of UFO's. They were shown to Eisenhower at Edward's Air Force Base. The church considered they would lose their following when the dimensions of the universe were uncovered. If this is true it is also shocking, but like politics, Religion has its darker side. As long as man's hands are involved Religion cannot be pure, because the impurity on man's mind corrupts the cause.

The most alarming policy of the Church of England in the last few years has been their move towards banning children from confirmation unless the parents are regular church-goers. This goes directly against the wishes of Christ that said; "Suffer little children to come unto me for theirs is the kingdom of heaven." It is also a very short-sighted policy considering church attendance is diminishing at an alarming rate.

You don't have to be a regular church-goer to be a good Christian. The pressures of life today exclude many Christians from attending church. That does not make them bad Christians and certainly should not be taken out on their children.

Religion should move into the nineties aiming to capture the attention of our young folk. How better than to sell off their worldly riches, jewels, art and land and invest in youth. In this way they will create a rebirth of Christianity and put our future on a hopeful path.

They can do this by setting up youth centres in the communities, not just to teach Religion but to give our youth a place to go other than the street corner. They should give our youth the leisure facilities they want rather than a preconceived programme. Then they will find the reward. Belonging.

Youth today is lost, out of work and with no apparent future. Is it surprising that they thieve, joy ride and take drugs? It's their only pleasure in a world that seems to have dealt them all the bad cards.

Our children have always been and still are our hope for a better world. Can the church step out of its traditional past and resolve the battles within, destroying its unity? After all the world does not care whether the preacher is a male or female, the message is what counts. The average Jew relishes the thought of eating ham or bacon yet he is strictly forbidden to do so by his synagogue.

The Roman Catholic is forbidden to use contraceptives and is therefore meant to practice abstention from intercourse except to create new life. These rules and many more besides are tools used by Religion to gain a hold over their followers and to discipline their lives. Unfortunately Us Folk too often seem to mimic the behaviour of sheep and follow without analysing the reason.

The new generation can change our ways and find a better way foreword. Youth is the challenge for Religion today. Is religion mature enough to realise the potential?

THE ARMED SERVICES

The Armed Services are an instrument of government to protect our land and its assets, and defend Us Folk from aggression in a cruel world. This is an aim fully supported by the majority of Us Folk. Where it is used to defend us against civil disobedience and insurrection, support depends on each person's view and is not so unanimous. Just think back to our boys that saved us from Hitler's mob. This should be enough to realise how lucky we are in Britain.

THE PARADE

You know, the British really do know how to throw a party, especially if the reason for the party is something about which they can be justifiably proud.

Heaven alone knows why world war two was allowed to happen. Reasonably, one would have thought that after the slaughter of the first war, a lesson had been learned. Clearly not. A five foot something corporal from that previous war ignored all the international treaties and arguments, formed a political party and eventually swept to power on the wave of nationalistic promises and secret terror.

Adolf claimed Austria, his homeland, and Bavaria, and there was a reluctant acceptance but then he turned his attention to Poland, Norway, the Netherlands and France. "Enough is enough," said Britain and told Hitler that if he didn't withdraw he'd be in trouble.

Adolf Hitler controlled everything up to the English channel. The British army, snatched from the beaches of Dunkirk, was bedraggled and disorganised. The Royal Navy was stretched in the Atlantic and the Royal Air Force had a meagre six-hundred aeroplanes. The British people had their backs to the wall. But I'll tell you something; the British are mild, gentle people but get their danders up and you'd better hide the good crockery. Well, Mr. Hitler laid out his dinner service and got the lot smashed in his face.

He thought he had it all his own way in the Spring, Summer and Autumn of 1940. He reckoned without the

121

courage and, very likely, innocent bravado of a group of young men who scrambled into Hurricanes and Spitfires and braved odds of four-to-one. He underestimated the British resilience: a very grave mistake. His airforce was cut to pieces in the skies above Southern England by a group of young men who were not more than a year or two out of puberty. He tried to bomb the British into submission but they went into the underground stations and sang songs like: "We'll meet again, don't know where, don't know when, but I know we'll meet again some sunny day." Also "Who do you think you are kidding Mr. Hitler, if you thought old England done?"

A rather plump old man in a black jacket and nineteen-thirties trousers, later, in an overall which became known as "The siren suit" stood up and waved his fingers in the air. "V for victory," he cried and the British were inspired. They came out of their underground protection, went backed to their bombed and often shattered homes and pushed their backs off the wall, defiant.

"Give us the tools and we will finish the job." The siren-suit told the Americans and Mr. Roosevelt answered the call. Sherman tanks poured into North Africa and General Montgomery chased the African Corps all the way across the desert. Then Italy fell.

By now the Japanese capture of Pearl Harbour had happened and the Yanks were into the war in earnest. Thousands and thousands of very young men from a country Britain only knew about from cinema screens joined other young men and climbed into landing-craft and waded ashore in the face of hostile gun-fire. It was 'D' day, nineteen-hundred and forty-four. It was June, the middle of the summer, but instead of basking in green shaded parks young men spilled their blood on the beaches of France. It only took those remarkable young men a year to get the job done.

Well, now those remarkable young people are old. They sit in wheel-chairs, lean on walking-sticks and have a rather confused look in their eyes. But, the weight of the medals which pull their civilian clothes slightly out of shape are evidence of their early commitment to the cause of freedom, democracy, call it what you wish.

I found myself standing beside one of those 'Old codgers.'

"Were you in the war?" I asked.

"Just a bit, just a bit," he said quietly.

My eyes fell to his jacket. Pinned to his coat was a row of medals proclaiming experiences in North Africa, Italy and Germany. One of those medals was a thin strip of purple ribbon below which hung a small, bronze cross. The words screamed at me: 'For Valour.'

My mouth opened. I looked at him. He appeared a mild mannered, old gentleman. I reached out and took his hand.

"Thank you," I said, "Thank you so very, very much."

Although the forces are split into Army, Navy and Air Force they work as a team to accomplish their duty to government. In a rapidly changing world their roll is constantly in need of reappraisal and the Gulf War has given a clear example of its adaptability. The demand of modern warfare requires a constant rolling back of perimeters. It is these changes that determine the use of planes, ships, tanks, artillery and all the modern weapons that can now deliver pin point accuracy in battle through the command and control systems. It was a major test between the Russian system installed in Iraq and the highly sophisticated system used by American command: this determined the result of the gulf war.

At the heart of modern combat we find command and control. It is generally accepted that this is the pivotal point between victory and defeat. Therefore it was interesting to see the airborne blitz of Iraq's command and control network guided by special agents inside Iraq. Until this was complete the conventional military attack did not proceed. This was a decisive factor in the low loss within the allied forces.

From that moment Iraq was fighting without co-ordination. Coupled with which, a crippled air strike capability, partly self inflicted by their tactical retreat to Iran for protection, hastened their demise.

So modern military control has moved, from a liaison job between headquarters and the field commanders, to an intelligence data bank constantly being updated.

This relieves commanders from analysing enemy deployment, a previously arduous task containing an element of guessing and often lacking in vital intelligence. It therefore let them plan their deployment of hardware and personnel, using their assets economically in relation to the intelligence data. This is why a country with a smaller army and less hardware can, with a superior command and control system, beat their adversary. The side that controls EW, (Electronic Warfare) or the spectrum, as it is called, will win the war.

All this is very different from our force's amateurism displayed in the first and second world wars. A time when rightful criticism can be heaped upon our

commanders and the almost careless way they sent their soldiers to their deaths.

Thankfully the command has passed to trained and intelligent men. In the past the most important qualifications were their family background and the public school they attended rather than their ability to command. Today our armed forces are the best in the World. Highly trained, highly motivated, and highly professional. They are backed by a group of specialised men, trained to the ultimate degree in their particular field to carry out special assignments in battle. A good example of which was the storming of the Iranian Embassy.

The SAS (Special Air Service) or SBS (Special Boat Service) are quite simply the best in the world. They did a dedicated task behind the lines in the Gulf, enabling the feed-back of vital intelligence and assisting the guidance of the 'smart' bombs for the pin point bombing raids.

The SBS were the first to land in the Falklands to wipe out the Argentine command and control system and again pass back intelligence.

These brave men, highly trained and motivated, are kept on an adrenaline run during their service in our special forces. It is to our shame that these men receive no help to re-adjust when they retire from this vital service. The problems they face are sometimes insurmountable. As with the war veterans and the war widows before them, our Nation, to its disgrace, has chosen to ignore their plight. These men, without help, can be time bombs when they enter civilian life. They need proper help to re-adjust. They deserve this help for the service they have performed for us all.

Behind the modern forces are the back-room boys who design and manufacture our weapons and develop the computer software to run our defence programmes.

Each company or military research academy rolls back the frontiers of knowledge, advancing our defence and therefore its structure, year by year.

Today the computer, with its specially designed software, is at the heart of our defence. It has become the most secret part of our whole military programme Defence into the nineties covers a whole field of defence linkage, encompassing EW command and control intelligence. It joins British forces to American forces in Britain to allied forces in Europe and NATO command, each gathering and sharing their intelligence. It is all fed into a central computer bank of enormous capacity. It is capable of gathering over a million pieces of intelligence in a second and analysing it in a similar time span. The analysis will advise deployment of hardware and personnel to best defend against enemy movements. This programme when complete in the late nineties will put us in a commanding position.

Out of necessity defence must look far into the future to enable it to crack the impossible barriers we find today. They probably know our next move but we will have to wait to find out what it might be. Some of our work is well ahead of the world, especially in underwater research.

Our technicians have developed a simulator that can seek, find and destroy a submarine hiding under the ice caps of the poles. The technology that achieves this remarkable development resembles scenes from Star Wars. Simulators are used to test warfare systems. Every possible scenario is programmed into the simulator to test the weapons ability in use. This is the ace of electronic warfare.

Defence realism must be updated to appreciate World changes. Nothing illustrates this more than the collapse of the Communist pack of cards. We must also tread with care. One step at a time, to ensure we are still defended in a changing world. The forces on their part should be prepared to accept change and adapt accordingly. It is hard for a proud regiment to face amalgamation. It is a hopeful sign that we are entering an episode in our history when we can genuinely afford a reduction in our Defence Forces. The rich reward from this should be used to clean up our environment. It could be our last chance.

Defence realism is what we need. A balance must be found to meet today's concord between East and West. The pot of gold at the end of the rainbow is worth the effort. Our next war will need all the resourcefulness we can muster to save the world's environment.

SERVICE WITH A SMILE (AFTERWARDS)

The smartly dressed lady in the little booth looked at my ticket, smiled cheerfully and said.

"Good morning, platform three. Have a good journey."

It was nice to see someone in uniform enjoying their work. Apart from school cap and blazer, the army was the only organisation I've ever worked for which provided free clothing and also provided a large pair of boots, something heavy to sling over your shoulder. They also handed over an assortment of destructive implements, some which you pointed, some which you threw and some whose purpose I never did discover. Then, as a preliminary to a much higher level of activity, offered instruction on how to march, run and frog-hop around a tarmacadam plot which on Saturday afternoons moonlighted as a hockey pitch. Other

delights included pre-dawn wakening by someone who thought he was Louis Armstrong but sounded more like a fog horn Freddie with flu. Five mile cross country runs followed by cold showers, beans, sausages and tea ladened with bromide.

Most of this entertainment was orchestrated by an honours graduate from the Marquis de Sade Academy with reciprocal views on parentage and a caustic wit sharpened by years of frustration suffered in trying to turn unruly boys into less unruly, more disciplined men. I recall one occasion, standing on parade, quietly scratching my backside. Eagle eye didn't miss a thing. He opened his mouth and bellowed, "That man. Stop scratching your arse. If you've got a sore throat, report sick." The Beaufort scale never recovered.

During those first few weeks of training nothing seemed to go right. Hurricane mouth would yell, "Right turn," a simple enough command, which often produced something resembling a free-for-all, as recruits fell over one another. Kit inspections were never good enough, and no matter how much cleaning you gave your rifle, there was always a speck of dust up the barrel. On the range the targets were always too small and too far away. Old chevron- sleeves would tell us that the safest place to be was in front of the guns. He never offered to prove it. Then, almost suddenly, a transformation took place.

One day we were a gaggle of near hopeless individuals. The next our pressed uniforms no longer hung like something on a scarecrow. Our backs were straight, our heads high and our responses to command sharp and slick. We stood to attention as one body of men, eagerly waiting for 'Our Boss' to inspect us. This was our graduation; our passing out. He who had inspired hate-at-first-sight walked slowly between the ranks and then came to stand in front. There was an unmistakable look of pride on his face, and for almost the first time since our initial encounter he spoke softly.

"Well, gentlemen," he said, "This is it. One more march round the parade ground and you'll officially be soldiers. Remember what you've learned here and add to that the knowledge you'll accumulate in the future. You've earned the right to that knowledge - use it wisely.

He was about to turn but hesitated.

"By the way, I'm proud of you."

The parade master yelled, "Quick march," the band struck up and off we went, arms swinging, eyes snapping to the right in unison, twice round the ground and into the mess for beer, sandwiches and soldiers farewells.

Someone once asked me if I enjoyed my army life.

"Not much," I replied, "people kept shooting at me."

"But it's a great life," they insisted, "free clothing, free accommodation and free food and travel."

I nodded, not wishing to disillusion him. Obviously, he hadn't heard that most of the travelling was done on foot, often in the rain. The accommodation frequently turned out to be a foxhole half full of water and shared by as many as could squeeze in. The food came cold out of cans and was shovelled-in with either a bayonet or bare fingers. True, the clothing was free but it wasn't long after setting out on the little walking tour before it became torn, wet, filthy, and if you were lucky, full of holes.

When all the jollifications were over, this organisation, which had provided the free clothing, took it all back. Goodness knows what they did with it. The cleaning and repair bill would have been double its worth. Still, I didn't mind. My experiences wearing other peoples clothing have been far from happy and I swore that day that the next uniform I wore would be a shroud.

THE POLICE

An emotive word that creates in some of us a warm feeling of protection and in others, not necessarily criminals, a feeling of arrogant mistrust and even hate. Why such mixed feelings?

Quite simply it is a case of judgement by experience or hearsay. Police are used to do political work in crowd control during strikes or demonstrations. This effectively alienates them from the strikers and their sympathisers. This is not their fault as they are carrying out orders essential for keeping the peace. Unfortunately in such situations their mere presence sometimes has the opposite effect.

A SIMPLE THOUGHT

Policemen and Policewomen are mostly young people with mothers, fathers and wives or husbands and in many cases young children just like you or me. They go about their daily business of protecting 'Us folk' the public. Most of 'us' are grateful that they do this. Some others of 'us' throw stones at them, yell and scream insults at them, stick knives into their stomachs and shoot guns at them and even kill them.

Does it surprise you that any decent copper gets a bit upset by the treatment of some of 'us'?

We are quick to assess and nearly always wrong to generalise in judging the Police.

The force is made up from several groupings each of which has its own particular job to fulfil. So what are these groupings?

THE BEAT BOBBY

The Beat Bobby is by far the largest group and is the man we see daily patrolling the streets in our wanderings. He is usually kindly, courteous and helpful. Ready to direct you to your destination, help you in distress and guide you across a dangerous road when you are old and frail. He also helps to stop crime. He is in constant contact with his base and can call on all types of back up if required. He can for instance check a suspected car to see if it has been stolen.

He gained the British police force the reputation of being one of the best forces in the world.

His involvement in the neighbourhood watch schemes has helped to add a feeling of re-assurance to communities, especially when crime figures are soaring.

The next section, backing up the patrolman, is the mobile policeman. The way some of these guys drive should be criticised. It is not worth risking injury to themselves or to innocent bystanders to reach the scene of a burglary. Consider this typical festive scene and you will see what the police have to cope with in the normal course of a day's work:

SAINT PATRICK'S DAY

It was just before quarter to twelve and the date was still March the seventeenth, fifteen minutes before the end of St. Patrick's night. Sean was holding me up from the left and I was holding up Sullivan at my right. We lurched out of the pub and went in search of a final quarter of an hour's adventure.

The street corner was not only a convenient piece of geography; it was, to our Guinness effected minds, a suitable open air music-hall. After 'Danny Boy,' 'Irish Eyes Are Smiling' and 'Does Your Mother Come From Ireland?', a pyjama clad resident had his complaints silenced by Sullivan with a wealth of language and volubility that had lights going on all down the street. Then, "Mee-Maw, Mee-Maw" and a blue uniform was getting out of a white car and asking us "What is going on here then?"

"Good evening Offisher," said Sean, "'Tis a beautiful night." Sean let go of my arm, straightened and fell backwards through somebody's privet hedge. The circle of mutual support that had kept us upright was broken. Sean was down, Sullivan began a short, involuntary stagger and I fell forward, clawing for something to break my fall. My hands closed around the policeman's trousers. I hung on and my fall was checked; but only checked. As the officer's braces stretched both his trousers and I succumbed to gravity and I found myself, chin resting on highly polished boots, staring up at a pair of white, red spotted under-pants. With admirable stoicism the constable reached for his notebook appearing to ignore the icy wind that must have been freezing his----knee-caps. "Can you stand up sir?" he said. "Of course I can stand up," and to prove the point I stayed exactly where I was. I did let go of his trousers and the braces catapulted the waistband upwards at orbital speed. As the crutch of his trousers met his groin the policeman lifted his heels and said, "Oh dear," in rather a soprano tone he probably hadn't used since he was eleven years old.

Meanwhile, his partner had got out of the car and was attending to Sullivan. He was showing tremendous patriotic enthusiasm with his rendering of, "An

American Landed In Eiren's Green Isle" whilst in an arm lock.

Help arrived for the police in the form of a white van with a red stripe down the side and bearing the emblem of the Metropolitan Police. A sergeant got out holding a ferocious Rin-Tin-Tin on what looked like an all too fragile chain. I tried to say "SIT" but there was a "h" in there and the dog understood and did it all over my shoes.

"Come along gentlemen," sergeant said and I knew from the tone of his voice that he and Rin-Tin-Tin meant it. I walked to the van as the more composed if not more sober of the drunken trio. Sean was carried, soporifically unaware of what was happening. Sullivan, still offering his bathroom imitation of Mario Lanza, had to be persuaded.

The desk sergeant was a friendly fellow and seemed to sympathise with us. However he still told us that we would be held over night and that we would be charged under some act or other that contravened some by-law or other. It is of retrospective interest that he never mentioned the words Pissed or Drunk.

We were not three-to-a cell, as I had always believed that was the type of accommodation incarcerated people suffered. No, I had a cell to myself and the room service wasn't too bad either. A policeman brought me a cup of canteen tea and we exchanged jokes before he went off to try to silence a still very voluble Sullivan.

"You would think that a self respecting drunk could get a decent nights sleep in a gaol cell," I yelled through the peep-hole in the door. It had no effect on Sullivan. He and Mario Lanza had a pact: Sullivan thought that he sounded like Mario and intended to advertise his belief. It wasn't until four o'clock that his strength and vocal cords gave out and he fell asleep.

Breakfast was a tin plate full of eggs, bacon, and beans with hot, sweet tea and was delicious.

Sunday morning and a special court hearing was convened. Being hung-over, un-shaven and confronted by a magistrate who had been summoned from his normal Sunday morning routine induces a humility of which Winston Churchill would have been proud.

They had convened the court to deal with a couple of people who had been caught trying to plant bombs in a local cinema. Also some thirty or forty youths who had used a football stadium as a battlefield, plus three, by this time very contrite, drunks. The company wasn't of my choosing but the situation most certainly was. I have always been the architect of my own downfalls.

I was always under the impression that I was a hunted man till I read this news flash in my paper one day. Now I realise I have helped to save the world.

SCIENTISTS CLAIM DRINKING MORE CAN SAVE THE PLANET.

'Drinking more whisky and beer could reduce the green House effect say scientists at the Edinburgh Science festival'.

You see: I told you so. Quite a few of us have been "tellin' 'em so" for years but nobody listened. Well, now it's official: all those elbow-bending, bar-propping, ice-tinkling, glass-emptying, eye-blearing

137

'Happy Hours' were not in vain. All that selfless hedonism suffered above and beyond the call is going to save the world.

"WE" knew it all along, of course, but don't imagine for one moment that we didn't suffer for our cause. All those hangovers, headaches, heart attacks and hallucinations were the pains of martyrdom to be borne with steadfastness. Those nights of fitful sleep in the backs of cars or in bathtubs or, simply, wherever we happen to fall down. Oh yes, how we suffered.

We faced more than a single foe. There were the mighty and fearsome Abstinence league blowing bugles and thumping tambourines and promising eternal damnation. The temperance society cavalry of ferocious ladies in tweed, thrashing and jabbing pointed umbrellas. Above all, we faced the awesome main battle force of mother-in-law, armed to the teeth with wagging tongues, shaking fists and "I told you so" missiles.

Most of our operations, from necessity, were covert. We would sneak through the dark riverside streets of the city to rendezvous in places like, 'The Tolling Bell', Waterman's Folly', and 'Dirty Dicks', where we sat in dismal corners, conspiratorially hugging glasses and planning a better future. Occasionally, we mounted an overt operation. Dressed as rugby footballers or soccer hooligans, small parties of specially trained men and women openly attacked the fortified citadels of conformity. There was a raid on a vicar's tea party where sergeant Drunkalot distinguished himself in an assault on the cider barrel. Who can forget corporal Tipple, who led a small group of volunteers into a market square and scattered the Salvation Army with their raucous rendering of "Nellie Dene." Our ranks are filled with brave people, both living and dead. We fought a long, hard war and even the heinous weapons used by the enemy such as liver cirrhosis (Which is

139

incidentally banned under the gin and tonic convention) failed to shake our resolve.

Now, at last, we've won. Science is to present evidence which will justify our long, hard struggle. Those of us who survived can honour our dead. Sergeant Drunkalot and Corporal Tipple will receive postumous VC's (Victuallers Cross) Major Martini and Lieutenant Lager will each get O.B.E.'s (Our Beer's Excellent) and myself will receive a knighthood for all the work I did between eleven in the evening till dawn.

Let there be peace between the knocker and the knackered and let both sides raise their teacups and their glasses in a toast to understanding.

THE TRAFFIC POLICE

Now there's a group we love to hate. We've all come across them and tried to spin them some yarn or three relating to the reason for speeding or parking where we shouldn't. It is no good. They have heard them all a thousand times over.

The truth is, Us Folk, when we get into a car it changes our personality. We turn into monsters who can't do anything wrong and excuse ourselves for all our misdeeds.

Idleness and mis-judgement of urgency make us park in the wrong places and drive faster than the regulated limits.

The planners must carry blame for parking chaos. Stupid speed regulations on some of our roads encourage us to break the law.

The police can only implement the law as it stands but carries the blame for useless regulations in so doing.

In particular the practice of wheel clamping and car

lifting should be regarded as totally useless and counter-productive.

When it was first introduced in the spring of '88 the idea was to penalise motorists so heavily that they would leave the car at home and come to work by public transport.

However the planners failed to see the upheaval this would cause.

I was a casualty of this ill-conceived policy in as much as my shop was in a street that bore the first thrust from the car snatchers. The street was bombarded by lifting trucks on a ruthless sustained drive to clear London of cars. The effect was so great that my shop lost a third of its trade overnight, and by the following year never recovered, despite every effort to reverse the situation. Even on a Saturday morning, when I tried to fit a battery to a car for a man in his seventies, these vultures tried to tow his car away.

Needless to say my shop ceased trading. I could not sell it as a going concern because of this blight, so I was forced to sell the lease alone and was therefore left with the stock. No compensation was forthcoming. Not even sympathy.

I was not the only one. Twelve other shops closed in my small area alone. This was a blow to small shop keepers but also a loss to the local community.

So why was this policy a failure? It did not think past penalisation, blaming the motorists for the long standing failure of the city planners. By clamping cars they remain at least three times longer in restricted parking places, causing a larger problem than the original offender.

By lifting cars, the lifting vehicles block the arteries of London causing far more blockage than the car parked illegally at the roadside.

The commercial aspect introduced to this policy insured that the roads with the most potential coupled with their proximity to the car compound dictated the roads that were blitzed by the snatchers. By using this combination they could maximise the profits to be made from this legalised theft. The treasury and the private contractors were certainly making a killing from it while Us Folk were being robbed.

So instead of using the weapon carefully to avoid obstruction it turned into a commercial grab, assisted by the police traffic section who label the cars to be lifted.

All this because our planners have failed in the past to face up to the parking problem head on. It is only arrogant politicians and police chiefs that suggest we leave our cars at home, when we have been encouraged to buy them and pay massive taxes to purchase and run them.

Us Folk, have the right to demand an adequate network of car parks to accommodate our vehicles within reasonable distance of work or our shopping centres. No other fudged acts are acceptable.

It is therefore wrong to blame the police for their part in this policy, except to say the chief constables could have advised against it as it would build a barrier between them and the public. The Department of the Environment and the local authorities are fully responsible and must clean up their act and face up to the parking problem. The police in the meantime must operate a damage control policy by executing their duty with reason and understanding especially when Us Folk blow a fuse!

Traffic wardens. Those wasps we hate are controlled by traffic division, although the police, like us, to believe they are a separate entity. Their sting still hurts. Us folk sometimes need a sting. It amazes me how none of us have been more than a minute or so when we discuss our ticket with the meter maiden. Most times it is a fair sting so lets face up to it and grit our teeth.

Planners, just give us our parking spaces and none of this will happen.

C.I.D. AND REGIONAL CRIME SQUAD

The CID is the crime buster, and the Regional Crime Squad tackles the larger jobs, including political crimes.

On the few occasions I have dealt with the CID I have found them to be very slow on the uptake. One example was when a strange event happened. A mini cab driver reported to his control that he was carrying two men who were going on to my shop to steal a car battery. This much he gathered during their ride in his cab. When they collected the third man he reported into his control who in turn informed the local police station. They took thirty-five minutes to cover one and a quarter miles to my shop. When they arrived they interviewed the manager who knew nothing about the planned robbery, and therefore told them he had not been robbed, at which point they left. Now it does not take the brain of Britain to realise that if the information came through a cab driver, the shop manager would not know what happened unless he happened to catch them stealing it. So the thieves got away with it, despite the fact the theft was reported before it was undertaken, giving ample time to catch the rogues red handed.

THE STOLEN CAR

The fact that this happened may surprise you. Nevertheless it did.

I arrived home at approximately twelve fifteen that night, slightly merry but able to stand, for which reason I took a cab. As I was about to unlock my front door I felt something strange about me. Yet I knew not what was wrong.

Looking around it struck me that my car was not parked in its usual place where I always left it.

At first I racked my brain to find if I had parked it somewhere else. Nothing came of it until suddenly the realisation my car had been stolen hit me like a ton of bricks. I rushed to the phone and called the police. An answerphone told me my local police station was closed and gave another number to ring. I rang and waited ages, till just as I was about to give up, someone picked up the phone the other end.

"Duty sergeant, can I help you?"

I went through all the details and then he informed me I should go down to the station in the morning to make a statement. In the meantime he promised to circulate the details.

In the morning I made the trip to the station as requested. Enquiring about my car, I was informed it was early days yet. Never a truer word was spoken in jest. After seven days and no news I decided to make another visit to the station.

As I approached, to my surprise my car was parked right outside the station, relatively unharmed except for the locks.

I ran up to the duty sergeant's desk and half shouted;

"Well done." I was halted by the sergeant who turned to face me; "Sorry I haven't got any news for you on your car, it takes some time to search the area. It's very large, you know."

"But...," I was halted in my tracks again.

"We have informed the full squad and they are keeping their eyes open for it. You must be patient."

"But..."

"No buts, there's a good man."

"I just wanted to tell you my car is parked right outside the station."

There was a stunned silence.

During the next week I was stopped six times and accused of stealing my own car!

Yes, the C.I.D does get their facts muddled but does it get better higher up the ladder? The regional crime squad was set up to fight organised crime and political atrocities more efficiently by being linked directly to the fountain of knowledge. The central computer. Yes, you would say, a good move to use the latest state of the art technology to beat crime. What have been the results so far?

Unfortunately too many cases have had to be reviewed because specialised evidence has proved to be suspect, or in extreme cases where evidence was cooked by the investigating team. It is a disgrace to our system of justice that this should happen and indeed take so long to correct. The C.I.D regional squads should be ashamed of the men that let it happen and deal with them harshly. If found guilty they should be dismissed from the force for bringing our justice system into disrepute. The IRA must be laughing themselves silly.

This has done irreparable damage to the force. So what went wrong? In a simple sentence; pressure to convict. That's no excuse, just the fact. All investigation teams are under police, political and media pressure to produce a quick result. They seem to ignore the procedures laid down for a conviction on hard evidence in favour of fudging and even forging statements and evidence. Unfortunately for them it can be exposed by modern technology. The method used when deciding to prosecute must be examined and a more satisfactory way found to ease the pressure on the investigators. From the outside it looks as if the police cannot get anything to stick. It will take a long time to repair this damage. In the meantime Us Folks pay for the police. Pay for the trial. Pay for the prisons. Then pay compensation for the prisoners released after their appeal. So it's a rotten deal. Get your act together and stop fudging it.

VICE AND DRUG SQUADS

If they (the politicians) de-criminalised prostitution we could control it and make sure it was as free from disease as possible. Then there would be no need for a vice squad. Just a check kept on outlets. It seems sense to me. The same reasoning applies to drugs. Drug trading is the second largest business in the world; only beaten by arms. Drink, a chemical drug, is by far the worst cause of illness and death within the drug scene. It is legal and there would be a civil war if we tried to change its status.

De-criminalisation would bring much needed control of the drug scene but most important of all it would take the criminal element out of drugs.

We will not beat the drug barons. The will and resources are not available. The drug barons are too powerful and resourceful.

By de-criminalisation of drugs, not only can you control quality and tax sale but you take the criminal out of the system as the high profits no longer exist. It is the criminals that push drugs outside our schools and on the large council estates. Remove them and the demand would start to level out and fall. Drugs create other crimes. Make drugs cheaper and control its strength and crime will fall.

Drugs create a breed of criminals that end up stealing for their fix.

A programme of de-criminalisation, coupled with better education at school level would show a far more satisfactory result than the drug squad could ever, with all their hard work, achieve. Judge Pickles agrees, so I understand, and he has the knowledge through the courts to analyse the position accurately.

So let's take the bullet and bite it. Who knows? the result could see the abolition of the drug squad and their work contained within the main force again.

THE CHIEF CONSTABLE

The chief constable controls his area and liaises between his head office and the local council. His task is to direct changes in policing as the local area requires. Unfortunately some politicians try to change their role to suit the shade of their politics. He needs his freedom to do his job properly.

Their work-load has become a public relation's exercise to such an extent that a re-appraisal of their duty would help to get them back where they belong:

fighting crime. A little less masonry and a little more office would help to guide their teams into a more successful future. There is one area that must be overcome and that is the obvious reluctance to go into some troubled areas. No area should be classed as 'No Go'. This is a negation of their duty and a sure path to anarchy.

SPECIAL BRANCH

Behind the main force we have the Special Branch, who deal with the grey area of political policing. They carry out state security and political work. This can include guarding heads of state on visits or detaining unwanted immigrants.

The work is secret from necessity, but sometimes it is used to hide blunders by government or the civil service, that should be public knowledge.

We need an independent body to watch over their work and check the excesses. There are too many question marks hanging over them, for example the untimely death of Hilda Morrell, the Peace Movement protester against nuclear power stations. Evidence on her death has been suppressed and D notices used to stop news about the manner of her death. Couple that with her success in highlighting bad safety standards in the nuclear industry and it becomes less difficult to suspect foul play by the security executive.

However much we approve or disapprove of her work this country is meant to have free speech, a corner-stone of democracy. Sometimes you have to wonder if our security services, both MI5 and special branch, believe in democracy or rely more on the silence of dissenters. Mrs Remington stated in her Dimbleby lecture that MI5 did not kill people it did not like and I believe that is now a true statement. So who does? Is it a private security company distanced from government's wrong-doings? This practice, if used, should be investigated and ceased forthwith as it breaks the law of the land.

Freedom of speech is an essential part of democracy and they better start to believe it.

The police disciplinary system, although much more thorough and searching than we are inclined to believe needs a complete overhaul. It should be independent. This is the only way you will get Us Folk to trust the result.

Make these changes and a new era of trust and regard will dawn for our force and the security services.

Two last thoughts on the police. It is a popular belief that the police are responsible for the decline in law and order in this country of ours. In particular they are blamed for the lack of action against juvenile crime plaguing this country, especially the drug related crime of the sub culture. I, myself blame this lack of action on the politicians, who shackled the police in their endeavours, by taking away the certainty of prosecution after the police had finished their paperwork on the crime. This was done by cynical changes in the Criminal Justice act, because the Thatcher government knew in the self inflicted recession brought about to reshape industry, the country could not afford an over-crowded prison service and drug related crime was targeted to receive a particularly easy ride.

A SHAMEFUL DECEIT

At the beginning of the political led recession an act of government folly was cynically planned that effectively stopped criminals being brought to justice. Surprisingly it was enacted by a Conservative government, the so called party of law and order. A decision was made to cut back on arrests and imprisonments and by doing so reduce court proceedings to save the cost during recession.

This involved changing parts of the Criminal Justice Act and introducing a new act, PACE (Police and criminal evidence act.). This act effectively cuts down arrests and it encourages the police to caution young offenders rather than charge them, whatever their previous record shows. It positively discourages the police from entering a charge as they find, after all the paperwork involved, they cannot make their case hold up in court due to all the new restrictions in PACE.

No wonder the police forces are disillusioned with their job. The frustration of seeing crime all around you, knowing who the culprits are but being incapable of responding, must be frustrating to the extreme.

All this at a time of recession when it seems everyone but the government know crime is on a fast increase but the majority of which is not even reported as people are totally sceptical about the authorities.

Juvenile crime is showing one of the largest single increases and drugs are the catalyst in this pattern.

Juvenile crime in particular is being treated as a no go area by our politicians who seem to think they can waive a magic wand when recession is over and crime will disappear.

In the meantime Us Folk have to live amongst these monster children, who by the time the recession ends will be hardened criminals.

The juvenile crime sub-culture must be laughing in our faces when they find they only get a talking to having been caught in a criminal act.

Does this government realise it has built time bombs all over the country which could explode at any time?

They have handed over whole sections of our community to juvenile anarchists, something that will take them years to correct.

When I realise that if we had sacked the chancellor before Black Wednesday we would have had adequate funds to fight crime, I know what I would have done.

When are the politicians going to listen to Us Folk in the real world and fight to reduce crime around us while teaching our juveniles respect for the society they live in.

Am I too cynical in thinking politicians do not want to solve real issues?

One thing is clear; the longer we postpone action the greater becomes the problem of juvenile anarchy.

Therefore it is wrong to blame the police for lack of action, or even the extraordinary way that those that were imprisoned were handed holidays on the state, to correct their criminal activities. This form of prisoner reform, applied by the social services, is a gross insult to the victims of the crime the person offended against, and spends 'Us Folks' hard earned money in a contemptuous manner. Take a look at these examples.

SOCIAL SECURITY

The largest spending agency in government, this monster is growing in demand by the minute, sucking

up our hard earned cash to support millions of people who we are told are disadvantaged and down on their luck. I for one would not deny the genuine claimant's their just dues, but how do we ensure that they get the help they need, to the exclusion of the vast army of scroungers that daily invade the social security offices.

Something has got to change radically in the near future or this ever expanding section of something for nothing cult will bankrupt Us Folk with its ever increasing demands.

It seems to me that our stupid governments have vied with each other to create a monster that has bred a whole culture of people that think it is their right to live off the system and milk it for all it's worth. This culture is quite apart from the genuine unemployed and could be identified and separated from them.

Unless government grab this thorn and disarm it the system will bring about a much more dangerous result that will totally alienate two sections of our society. Us Folk can no longer pick up the increasing tab of social security and can see its future, if left alone, causing us to revolt en-mass against its power through government to bankrupt us.

Let's take a look at two sections of our community that now believe it is their right to use the state to finance their lives. These very people return nothing to society and you will see sections that totally abuse the original purpose of the social security system.

A DANGEROUS BABY BOOM

Question: What group has risen four hundred percent in twenty years and increased the cost to the

156

taxpayer, that's Us Folk, from two billion pounds to seven billion a year and is still rising out of control?

Answer: Single, unmarried mothers.

In my job I come in contact with this group of social security experts daily. It is therefore surprising to realise we are talking about young ladies aged between fifteen and twenty-four, generally lacking in adequate education (mostly their fault for not taking advantage of education they received) or moral standing. They have left school and found their ability to hold a job wasted by their lack of interest in their school studies during their education, making them virtually unemployable. They have found an escape route within the framework of our social security system which ensures them a roof over their head and money in their pocket.

Yes, priority on housing lists are given to one parent families so all they have to do is get pregnant and they can get the flat their parents had to wait years to obtain as well as cash assistance. This help was designed to assist divorced or widowed one parent families but has been flooded by this new generation of escapees from parental control. In many cases their parents have actively encouraged them to fall pregnant as they realise otherwise they will be a constant burden to them when they were hoping for assistance towards the family living costs. Girls have been known to sleep around with anyone willing to share one night stands till they fall pregnant and in so doing did not know who the father might be. All the knowledge about this abuse of the social security service is readily available to all girls still at school passed on by word of mouth and it is obvious to me it is getting more sophisticated as they learn new ways of milking the system.

The next stage begins at birth. Now it is surprising to me that social securities seem reluctant to identify the abusers who present themselves as single parents that are homeless as in my humble opinion, if parents of that girl had genuinely thrown her out it would have been when she became pregnant not after she had the child. Therefore the application for housing priority, which applies to single parents could easily identify and exclude this obvious form of abuse of state subsidies.

It is absolutely absurd that this arrogant section of the sub-culture actually believe it is their right to priority housing and state handouts when they have wasted their education and made no contribution to state funds.

Yet our state, in its infinite wisdom, does just that for these people. Isn't that just fine, Us Folk work our butts off to afford our lifestyle and are taxed to the hilt to pay for the lazy brigade.

Now I am the first to admit that my broad statements are a pattern example. Each case has its own individual characteristics and mix of elements but the vast majority follow a similar pattern.

They come from run down council estates. They are educated in the worst twenty-five percent of stateschools. Many come from single parent families with little or no discipline or the worst from over imposed restrictions. Their parents have struggled through life either on low pay or unemployment benefit. Through their education and home estate environment they have associated with the juvenile criminal elements surrounding them and their children are likely to be fathered by one of the juvenile criminals from the sub-culture I have described elsewhere. They only live for the day, ignoring the future and in many cases spend most of their social security payments to buy drugs.

The tragedy of this selfish attitude is the future of the children and that and that alone is where our sympathy should be focused.

The third stage is where the state begins its subsidy for life. The girl will claim homelessness, stating she has been thrown out of home. This is a big lie in most cases as the parents are totally involved in the deceit and the girl will commute between the halfway house or council approved bed-sit and her parents home regularly in the next six to nine months while waiting for priority housing. This is another time when the social security could check the validity of the claim of homelessness, but they don't. I know this is true because I carry them in my taxi. I also know in the vast majority of cases their has been no breakdown between parent and child. Therefore it is not a valid case of homelessness.

One girl I carry openly admits a family decision was made that she would become pregnant. She is now in a council bed-sit and commutes regularly between it and her parents home by taxi. Her mother is adamant it is her daughters right to housing and state handouts so she may exist without work for the foreseeable future. The mother bases this on the fact she has paid her stamp and is therefore entitled. This is not true as it only covers her own children till they get their own stamp at the age of eighteen.

Another girl I carry has a boyfriend but he is in and out of jail regularly. She has had her child and has been re-housed in a brand new house. Her boyfriend is a drug addict who steals to pay for his habit, and beats her up when she complains, or refuses him her money. Her brother is in and out of jail, but not so much recently as the police are not arresting his type so much now. However he still does thieving to pay for his habit, and he also joy rides for kicks.

So I can go on case after case.

This is a window into the underclass or sub-culture that has grown so rapidly and is now threatening our

society. If it is allowed to continue it will overrun our lives as well as bankrupt Us Folk with unbearable taxes.

Unless we make some radical changes to our welfare state and rethink our acceptable duty to the under-privileged, who must be protected, our welfare bill by the next century will be unaffordable.

TO MAKE THE PUNISHMENT FIT THE CRIME

I find nothing wrong in sending young offenders on character-building holidays. One recent offender was sent to the valley of the Kings where he saw the pyramids, and took a boat ride down the Nile. It must have been awful for him, and just because some people that made the same trip have had to save hundreds of pounds over probably, several years, is no excuse for condemning the local council for such an enlightened method of solving its crime problem. I decided to phone the local council to congratulate them.

"I would like to talk with the person responsible for sending the young offender to Egypt in order to stop him committing more offences. I would like to congratulate him."

There was a long silence.

"Hello," I said, "are you there?"

"Yes, yes, er just a moment, I'll connect you with our Mr...." The phone crackled and I didn't catch the name.

"Hello," voice at council end said, "may I help you?"

"Well, I don't need any help, I'm just phoning to congratulate you on your enlightened method of crime prevention. Sending that young man to Egypt was inspirational."

162

There was a choking sound at the other end.

"Are you all right?" I asked.

"Oh yes, thank you."

He seemed to be spluttering and I assumed that, being a modest man, he was overcome with emotion.

"But, but the press..."

"Don't pay any attention to the newspapers. What do they know? They suggested that he ought to be in prison and just because he'd stolen all those cars and broken into all those houses and smashed all that property. The press is so insensitive."

"But public opinion..."Again I had to cut him short.

"Pooh to public opinion. Just because the poor misunderstood boy did all those dreadful things to other people doesn't mean he's bad. Just because he spat at his fellow travellers and made their holiday miserable, they shouldn't condemn him as anti-social."

"Do you mean that?" he asked.

"Of course."

"We must meet for a drink," he said.

"I'd love to," I said, "I wish to discuss spending several thousands of pounds of the tax payers money on another character-building exercise.""What's that? he asked, bursting by now with enthusiasm.

"How about taking the next offender on another trip to the desert. We'll introduce him to some Arab friends of mine who will peg him to the ground, cover him in something sweet and watch as the ants and snakes and scorpions crawl all over him. If that doesn't solve his problem, nothing will."

The telephone went dead.

THE CULTURE THAT NEEDS
A CURE

Suddenly the politicians have woken up to the violence around us, while the civil service builds round the problem a man managed wrapping of secret discussion, that succeeds in doing nothing but produce useless reports that use up our rain forests.

Oh yes, they talk enough when action is required, but talk is idle without correctly directed response.

I claim to know the root cause of juvenile crime and how to cure it. Are the politicians mature enough to accept the cause and order the action to stop the crime? Is the James Bulger factor powerful enough to move politicians past talking and into action? I see crime around me daily in my work. I am a taxi driver.

The cause is not a single one but several. Three are however predominant, and if cured would isolate the rest. The first is the direct result from a deliberate local government policy, encouraged by parliament and aided by social workers and the courts. It was started in the seventies and by the late eighties had grown to an unacceptable level, demonstrated by juvenile violence experienced today.

The mistake was to house the problem families on remote or run down estates as a containment policy, allowing them to misbehave within their area without too much police harassment. Thus the local authorities built the time bombs that are exploding up and down the country. With this senseless policy they have

164

created a whole sub-culture that has total disregard for property, society and the rule of law that is the thin line that keeps us from anarchy. It was this sub-culture that killed young James.

The same sub-culture ran over and killed a father on his way home by bike. This was the result of joy-riding for kicks in a stolen car while, most likely, under the influence of drugs.

That leads me to the second cause: drugs. The sub-culture uses drugs to provide its kicks and tune the nerves in preparation to steal cars, joy-ride and even torch the car when they have finished with it.

Cannabis resin and speed are the most common drugs used by the sub-culture. Drug dealers can be found on all problem estates, some as young as ten years old. Most users do drugs for their kicks. Dealers do it to pay for their own habit.

Those that don't deal end up thieving to pay for their habit. The more they get hooked the more they steal to pay for their next fix, and which ever course they choose they all end up breaking the law daily. If you study the official figures for robbery over the last twenty years, since the sub-culture was created by our planners, the figures have risen between 1970 and 1990 by a staggering six-hundred percent. That has to be an item for the Guinness book of records. Our planners were probably knighted!

However, despite this alarming rise in theft the police force has barely increased in numbers, prosecutions have actually fallen, and prisons have shown signs of emptying. This is, I hasten to add not the fault of the police force, rather the result of a cynical decision by government to save money in our prisons and massage the crime figures at the same time. Us Folk all know when politicians say crime is down that it only means the criminals are being allowed to get away

with their crimes, and that the figures should really be showing a fast increase in crime. This situation is now so bad that Us Folk don't bother to report crime anymore.

When I have asked members of the sub-culture why they commit crimes they say they can earn up to one thousand pounds for two hours thieving. Why should they work all week for peanuts, even if they are lucky enough to get a job? Morality was never taught to them at home.

They mostly admit they thieve to pay for their drug habit and also out of boredom. They have no fear as the chances of getting caught and banged-up are small.

The third cause is directly controlled by government and the economy. The government, because of its command of the economy and the prejudice it displays in the manner it manages it, must be responsible for the damaging effect on our national prosperity. The result of a generation and a half of recession or near nil growth is seen in the unemployment figures.

So with these factors in mind how can we change the ball game and tip the scales against the sub-culture.

First attitudes have to change within government. They must be prepared for a massive re-think to solve the problem including a change of direction on housing policy.

Where drugs are concerned they have two options. Firstly they could declare an all out war on the drug trade. That will entail doubling the number of custom's officers to enable them to search a substantial part of imports and passengers entering the country. The police will also need to be strengthened to cope with the increase in drug related crime. They need their powers of arrest restored to hit the dealers hard. The public must play their part by exposing anyone they know who is dealing in drugs, why not a drug watch programme?

It would also require a change of sentencing within our courtroom system. To this end the police and Criminal Evidence Act 1992 must be drastically altered or scrapped altogether to free the police to arrest the dealers. The police would then have the confidence to do the job they are prevented from doing under the constraints of the act. So released, they could sting the traffickers and dealers. The courts must be advised to lock them up for long, hard sentences but with the enlightenment of the environment around them as a rehabilitation course.

If our government is not prepared to fight the drug trade with all its power, because of cost in the present economic climate, there is only one other course to take, they must legalise all straight drugs and hand out life sentences to dealers distributing the dangerous new breed of mixer drugs that are lethal.

By legalising drugs they become available through licensed outlets, as is the case with the drug alcohol. Strength would be marked clearly on the packet and usage advised.

This will effectively remove the criminal element from drug dealing as the big money would no longer be on offer. It would stop the drugs be pushed to children at our schools, on the council estates, in dance halls and in and outside certain pubs. These are the places the sub-culture buy their fix. The sub-culture, given more time, will destroy our society as we know it and ruin many innocent lives along the way.

One side of the political divide states unemployment has no effect on the behaviour of the unemployed. The other side claims the sub-culture is a direct result of rising unemployment.

Both sides, as usual, have figures to prove their argument and in part both sides have half truth on their side as it all depends how they present their case. Such is politics.

The British economy has been held down, in all but recession, for the best part of the last fifteen years. This has led to urban depravation to such a degree that whole areas have fallen into decay. This alone creates the bed for the seed of the sub-culture to grow and thrive, fertilised by hopelessness of the environment. It is therefore not surprising that the inmates of such a prison revolt against society.

Failure by chancellor after chancellor to solve the economy's problems leaves Us Folk in despair while our society crumbles around us. Unless our economy can be kick-started the finances required to combat the sub-culture will be unavailable to solve the problem.

That is why, with regret, I have to conclude the government will deliver a statement 'Full of sound and fury, signifying nothing.' I hope I am proved wrong.

FOREIGN POLICY

Nowhere is the Civil Service more entrenched than in the Foreign Office. No Foreign Minister can make a decision without first clearing it with his senior Civil Servant in fear that he might drop a clanger. Civil Servant,s rule.

It has been voiced the reason Mrs. Thatcher finally lost the control of her party's mind, is because she went against senior advice from the civil service. The disagreement was over the policy for Britain's role in the EU. It is highly probable they master-minded her demise through a simple whispering campaign in high places, although I believe it was initiated by Jaques Delors. If they did plan her downfall it shows the strength and deviousness of the civil service. It was a tragic end for someone who fought this Goliath so hard. It shows all of us she could walk over the unions and some say even walk on water, but she was no match for the Civil Servants.

Although appointments are made in foreign posts that promote prominent citizens to figure-head offices such as ambassadors, they exist by co-operation with the civil servants that surround them. If they stray off the narrow path of obedience they are soon the subject of a whispering campaign and replaced by a more obedient person. As this work usually ends up in honours they usually comply.

Our quaint and old-fashioned honour's system, designed to acknowledge people who give tireless service to the nation and its people, is somewhat tarnished when you realise anyone who hangs onto high office in the Civil Service for long enough will get honoured. This also applies to politicians who serve their party. For instance did you know the chairman of the London Conservative association, having served his term of office, is automatically put forward for a knighthood? Somewhat takes the gleam off the gong, doesn't it?

The Foreign Office is ruled by Civil Servants born to rule and trained to maintain the services' status quo. There is some compromise to modern methods. Computers have replaced the typewriters but the thinking has not changed to adapt to the modern information based professionalism required to promote Britain abroad. Indeed, because the ideology is borne of old fashioned thinking they frequently get their policy replies wrong.

Although the Victorian attitude that everything that Britain does is best has long since died in the real world outside the foreign Corp., the perpetrators of ourforeign policy cling onto this arrogant attitude, failing to realise the people are too street wise to fall for such a hollow jingle. It is because of this approach that many of the trade exhibitions throughout the world fail to appreciate the British display. The reason is they have already been exasperated by the trade consuls' arrogant stance and patronising superiority. It is slowly changing but it needs a booster.

It really is time our Civil Servants realised we sell our products if they are the best and if the price is right in comparison to our competitors. The word 'IF' is all important.

The extravagance of our foreign outposts is well documented. The top Civil Servants surround themselves with all the imported comforts and use any excuse, cultural or commercial, to arrange lavish receptions emulating the opulence of years long gone. It seems their standards were set at the time of the wealth of the Raj and they are reluctant to forgo them.

The practice of using the diplomatic bag hides many of the luxuries ordered by these lords of protocol and lavish living. They abuse the diplomatic pouch by using it for their luxuries. They transport their Stilton, port, Madeira and claret and all their luxuries this way to our furthest outposts, not to mention Grouse in season of both kinds!

No wonder most of them don't look forward to returning home from their assignments. It's like coming down to reality with a thud.

Spying is mostly carried out by embassy staff. This is usually done under the guise of cultural, commercial or military attaches. In smaller countries this may be concentrated on commercial outlets and trade development.

In more important Embassys full scale military and commercial spying is the most important function after ambassadorial political duties.

The embassy spy is a very special breed of person. He is highly motivated by patriotic belief. He will glean any knowledge he can to help our side in times of strife.

Unfortunately the other side is also carrying out this practice and is better equipped for the job. These spy plants are attached to MI6 and combine to make a network of world-wide coverage. This is the grey area of the service and from necessity the actual details of their operations remain secret as indeed they should.

The Civil Service should be made accountable for their actions and answerable to an independent watch-dog when things go wrong. This should be coupled with a much better control over expenses. It is needed especially in Brussels where expense sheets read like bank audits.

Let's for a moment consider a breakdown in diplomatic endeavour and where it might lead. A picture will form in your mind that will explain the cunning and strength of our Civil Servants in the foreign office.

RULE BRITANNIA

Britannia Island was one of those freaks of nature that defied world evolution. Barely a mile across and seven miles long it shunned nature in its attempt to survive in an area of cruel seas and cold climates. Bordering on the seas of the Arctic, lashed most of the year by icy winds, yet it still existed. Ice caps could be seen drifting by on their way to warmer waters and disintegration.

Its main inhabitants were penguins and seals who used its shores to shelter from the cruel seas and undertake the propagation of their species.

Like any island it drew the adventurer to its shores. Its first recorded visitor in the 18th century had been a British explorer. He landed on its beach, his vessel having been holed by floating ice. It was the practice to raise the flag and claim the island as British territory.

Since that time Musthavia has disputed its ownership. As the nearest land mass their claim has validity.

However, the argument went on without solution and in the meantime a weather observatory was built for World shipping forecasts. This brought with it other settlers, hardy sheep farmers and a small group of ornithologists. In total thirty-eight people settled and gradually a further ten Musthavians came to help care for the sheep and earn their keep.

Diplomatic exchanges have flowed since then but the matters were never resolved. It made sense to hand over administration to Musthavia. The island was supplied by them; the islanders sold most of their produce to them and relied on their help in time of need. Although they were one hundred and fifty miles away, Musthavia was the nearest land.

However political endeavour and Foreign Office manoeuvring had kept the argument alive till now. A political change of direction now seemed certain to alter this trend.

A settlement was certainly against the wish of the Foreign Office and an urgent meeting was held to direct the next move.

At a closed meeting at the Foreign Office it was decided that this outpost of the foreign office should be maintained at any cost.

To achieve this the Foreign Office leaked a report that on first testing an oil exploration team had found rich reserves off shore from Britannia island. This had an immediate effect. The government back-tracked.

174

What came next was entirely predictable. The Musthavian government sent an ultimatum threatening action if the government did not continue negotiations. The British government, with advice from the Foreign Office, refused. The Musthavians sent a task force of fifty men and captured the island. The British announced they were sending a two-thousand strong force to re-capture the island.

It was a brave announcement, fully supported by press and television, because once a decision is made we British always fall in behind our leaders. The press built it up as a crusade to support Us Folk in a far away land. This had a uniting effect and our country went to war as one.

It took six days to muster the force and get our airborne troops to Britannia Island. Musthavia, in the meantime, landed eight thousand troops, almost their entire army, on this postage stamp of an island.

When our troops arrived their strategy was brilliant.

First destroying the enemy command and control, then landing on three fronts and forming a pincer movement on the Musthavian forces. The skills of our forces were too much for the larger Musthavian army, who after fighting a hard retreating battle, finally surrendered on the third day.

Our side lost two soldiers in battle and the Musthavians one hundred and twenty-eight. Having disarmed the Musthavian forces we allowed them to return home.

So what happens now? We had won the day; but the situation hadn't changed. The government still had an island that was un-economic to administer and now additionally had to be defended to protect thirty-eight citizens of GB and countless penguins and seals.

Well, first things first. Medals were awarded to the soldiers for great courage, one posthumously to a soldier who died leading an advance against the enemy under heavy fire. A defence force five hundred strong was established, and all necessary equipment supplied to feed and house them in reasonable comfort.

The grass airstrip was inadequate for the increased traffic so a tarmac runway and hangers were built to cope with the new situation.

The cost of defence rocketed, by-passing all estimates.

After spending over one billion pounds on installing a defence system, it was estimated that it would cost two hundred and fifty million pounds per annum to administer.

This was the cost to maintain thirty-eight passport holders and a desolate strip of land. The residents could have been re-housed on rich farmland in England for a fraction of this cost.

Did I hear someone say 'Beware of beginnings!' or were you too patriotic?

The Civil Service and particularly the FO had their way.

They retained their outpost and increased its manning by seven hundred and fifty permanent and two hundred and fifty part time Civil Servants. Yes, it was a great victory for the FO, but cost us folk dearly.

It was just today the newspapers carried a small article to say the oil exploration off Britannia Island had ceased as the quality and flow were insufficient for commercial exploration.

The most startling news this century has been the collapse of the Great Soviet Union. It amazed the world with its speed and thoroughness. Here is a plea from the new Russia that should be headed if a return to the old Russia or worse is not to happen.

REVOLUTION WITHOUT AN END

Once upon a time there was a Tsar of all Russia. He ruled his folk by demand and kept the people poor so he and his friends could live a high life of luxury. He was a weak leader and when the time of testing came he knew little of life to contain the peasants anger. They saw the Tsar spending their money like water while they were taxed to supply the rubles to pay for his extravagance.

So Us Folk, the poor but honest citizens, rose up against the Tsar and won a glorious battle against the armies of the Tsar. Our leaders formed a peoples party based on Communist principles inspired by Carl Marx and Trotsky. Our president promised us equality and assured us the state would supply our needs. It sounded a perfect ideology. Like most perfect theories the policy failed when human elements of greed, jealousy, desire, and lust for power took over government. Under Lenin they aimed to control Us Folk and made us subservient. They imposed rule by decree not by democratic vote. A one party state was imposed, denying us a choice.

To control Us Folk from revolt the secret service was given unlisted powers, to guide us into submission to the cause and those that did not follow the party line were cruelly treated in experimental prisons with immoral powers.

The church was suppressed. Our freedom to travel was removed. We became prisoners in our own homes and those that erred from the party line were thrown out of work.

Freedom of thought was suppressed and spies were used in our workplace and accommodation to report to party units in each town of the way we spoke about authority. We couldn't even trust our own children as they were also grilled at school about our attitudes. Life was a living hell made worse by the lack of necessities in the shops. One day there would be no bread. Next maybe soap was on short supply, queues everywhere.

Plenty was always round the corner but the inefficiency of the Communist regime installed to control our industries, agriculture and transport were so badly managed by the party faithful, and corruption was so widespread we folk were left with inadequate services.

We had a long line of leaders who came through the party system. Lenin, who found it necessary to build the KGB into the ruthless state control system it became, spending most of its energy on internal control soaking up our money once again.

Then Stalin, the butcher, arrived. He personally ordered the deaths of so many of us folk. The war came and Stalin supported the Western allies against the fascist dictator, Hitler. After the war he was granted a ring of satellite states to form a communist buffer around the borders of Russia. He then set about imposing communism with its suppression on his newly gained allies.

Thus Us Folk from Eastern Europe from 1946 on, have lived in fear of our lives. Suppressed by terrible forces when we stepped out of line, as our Czech folk did, led by our hero Dubcek, no one ever believed we would escape the shackles of communism.

Khrushchev was now head of our Soviet empire. A hard man who started to spend our national reserves on armament, ignoring the desire of the people to improve their living standards, in favour of a drive to become the largest stockists of nuclear power in the world. Our army and naval superiority was already established with more planes, tanks, and submarines than the western allies combined. Khrushchev wanted our nuclear presence felt as well, and in doing so in Cuba, brought us within hours of world war three.

All this time Us Folk were confined behind the iron curtain, unable to experience the advancement in living standards on the other side.

Occasionally people would escape or be shot trying to cross the forbidden borders. Nowhere was it more difficult than at the Berlin wall.

Then there was another purge in our political structure. This time Khrushchev lost his presidency and a few presidents later Mikhail Gorbachev came into power. At first he appeared to be from the classical mould of suppression, an Ex KGB man.

Not this man, he was different. He had an impeccable education. He was also the youngest leader to take control of the Soviet Union and had a modern and beautiful wife.

For the first time I had a feeling of hope. He made an immediate hit with the press and showed genuine desire to come to agreement on world disarmament, when he had assessed the future of the Soviet Union.

Gorbachev was above everything, even party loyalty, a realist. He knew the nuclear arms race was bankrupting his union and putting enormous strain on the thin line he had to tread to avoid a peoples revolt against deteriorating living standards.

His industries were performing badly. His agriculture was always down on forecasts and his transport and infrastructure was crumbling into disrepair. The military machine was taking all the available money. He also knew that America had won the race to control space, while Russia established expensive space stations. America had set up a satellite defence system called Star Wars giving the West undeniable control in space. Worst of all, Russia had nothing to compete with the command and control systems of the Western technology.

AND SO, THE SOVIET UNION OUSTED COMMUNISM WITH ITS POLITICAL SKULDUGGERY, REPRESSION OF TRUTH AND MANIPULATION OF THE PEOPLE, REPLACING IT WITH DEMOCRACY........ AND....ER....... CIVIL SERVANTS.
FAIRY STORIES

Meanwhile the world disarmament talks progressed, but slowly.

Gorbachev knew he must either overtake the Western intelligence collection, command and control, or cease the cold war. The financially bankrupt state of the Union gave no other option. Defence had bankrupted the Soviet Union.

First he tried to steal the secrets of command and control, but failing this he had no alternative but to play his last desperate card. He announced the opening of the Berlin wall to an astonished world. A master stroke for world peace, it was claimed.

It was however a desperate last attempt to save the Soviet Union from ruin. He hoped that the return to democracy, a treasured desire of Us Folk throughout the Eastern block would end at the borders of the States of Russia. At first it did. East Germany embraced democracy followed by Poland, Hungary, Czechoslovakia, Yugoslavia and even the autocratic states of Bolivia and Albania. They all fell to the uncontrollable demand for democracy. Communism, all at once appeared to be a paper tiger. We began to get excited in the Soviet Union as first Yeltsin then others demanded a path to democracy.

Gorbachev resisted but it was obvious he would not use force against his people. His old guard communists panicked at this weakness, in their eyes, and put him under house arrest away from Moscow.

This was Yeltsin's chance. He stormed the parliament buildings, arresting the hard line communists and sent a convoy to release Gorbachev. Success was his and it wasn't long before Gorbachev bowed out, leaving the leadership to Yeltsin who was, for the first time in eighty-five years, the democratically elected President of the Union of Russian states.

One attempt was made by the old guard communists to remove Yeltsin from power but democracy won the day.

So how is it today I feel ill at ease? Cheated once again of my chance to improve my lot. Well, Yeltsin's reforms to turn us into a market economy have faltered, sabotaged to a large extent by the old guard communists still in parliament and in top positions within our industrial structure.

The euphoria of freedom unanimously expressed by Us Folk on learning of our move to democracy after eighty-five years of communist torture has died down, replaced by a new feeling of lack of direction, leading to despair. Some are even saying we were better with the devil we knew.

That is not so, but evil influences are gaining ground, an example of which is the evil fascist ideas of mad Vlad. His ability to rouse the people is frightening, bringing back memories of Hitler.

This is not what Russia wants. Hope and progress is. I say to the Russian people be patient. It took seventy years for communism to totally suppress us, so give democracy a decade or two to repair the damage. I beg of you be patient.

To our new found Western friends I ask for understanding. Don't desert us now. Help us to democracy and to overcome the evil forces that flock into a political vacuum to grab what they can regardless of the chaos they leave in their wake. If we are to succeed we need your understanding, your expertise and your guidance. Please help Us poor Folk dispel the threat of autocracy.

In hindsight we do not seem to have moved far since the revolution. All we had then, and cling to now is hope. Please help us save our fragile hope from destruction.

The Tsar, then the communists have held Us Folk down for over one-hundred years. Democracy is our only hope to change our lives for the better.

THE TAX MAN

At the mere mention of this word our stomachs turn to jelly and we start to cringe. This man has the power to turn normal people into gibbering idiots at a stroke of his pen.

With the precision of a butcher making the most of a lean and ill fed carcass he can carve our meagre earnings into portions and distribute them legally amongst the fatted cows at the Civil Service. His power is absolute, and his compassion is non-existent. He can pry into our private lives with his scalpel to open up closed chapters and extort his pound of flesh. The more you protest the more likely he is to add another slice of your assets to his feast. He can drive grown men to tears and reduce families to homelessness.

The extraordinary thing is that in a large number of cases he finds that when your accounts are submitted for the following year, he refunds the ton of flesh he extorted from you because he over-taxed you in the first place.

By this time you could have been forced to work overtime to pay his bill. Sell your treasured antique collection at a rock bottom price or even lose your home and wife through impossible debts.

Does he express sympathy or compensate you for your demise? No, he does not. Instead, after you have paid off his excessive charges in instalments he sends you a bill for interest on his loan. Try to get this

refunded after he has returned your money and he will just laugh at you. What a stupid, clumsy, irresponsible and totally unfair system that allows him to do this to Us Folk. I know. It has happened to me. It seems to me that large corporations with vast profits can, with clever accountants and an offshore company or three, end up paying a pittance in tax through clever manipulation. They perform acts Us small Folk can't emulate as we cannot afford this corporate style accounting.

Many large companies avoid their share of the tax burden this way. The clever people at the revenue don't seem interested or able to penetrate their corporate shield to surgically remove their tons of flesh. Our burden could be less if they were made to pay their share.

It takes a certain type of person to join the revenue. He must have a total distrust of his fellow human beings. Regard everyone as a cheat and a crook. Be able to endorse heavy penalties without a blink of the eyes. Enjoy an interview with a taxed man to the point where the man starts crying. At this time he supplies him with a tissue made from re-cycled tax demands adding an extra five percent to his tax estimate.

Yes, he has to have a skin of rhinoceros hide and an evil mind. The truth is the majority of Us Folk don't try to fiddle. When we put in our returns the evil mind of the Tax man thinks everyone fiddles and they add a fiddle factor to our assessments.

His powers to search have become intolerable to the honest man. Surely the Tax man should have to prove dishonesty to a judge or magistrate before he has the power to remove our files and rummage through our lives? We badly need a people's charter to protect us from excessive meddling in our private lives.

Then there are the forms. The endless stream of forms that are churned out like butchers' sausages for us to fill in and return. Unless you make a copy each time you can easily get caught out giving the wrong information: especially if you don't quite understand the questions.

You remember that Peruvian railroad announcer that worked at the local council? He moonlights at the tax office and is in charge of form complications. He single-handedly confuses the nations' form fillers and himself for good measure.

THE TAX MAN COMETH

I am really rather an easy-going person. Friendly, jovial and a good mixer, so I'm told. At least I was, until that fateful day when that brown envelope, without a cellophane window, came crashing to the floor through my letter box.

Now there is only one thing worse than a brown envelope with a cellophane window and that is one without. They cease to have windows when the people the other end stop using computer mailing and standard letters. This happens when they are getting serious over money and are about to take action.

I didn't know all this at that point, so I opened it. I suddenly turned a different hue. First I went red then a mauve blue and then my legs gave way. It was a final demand for eight thousand five hundred and seventy eight pounds and sixty four pence payable by return, or else. Typed and signed and not run off a computer.

I staggered to the drink's cupboard. A stiff treble brandy repeated three times just about brought me back to reality. A habit to which I was not accustomed at nine thirty in the morning. My senses blurred

186

quickly and when I came round I felt as if a sledge hammer had hit me. The letter, still in my right hand brought my recollection back efficiently.

There must be some mistake, I thought. However, my name-R. Smith in black and white, and my address, 3 Groomfield Walk, were clearly typed at the top of the letter. No, there was no mistake. What had I inherited that could possibly bear over eight thousand inheritance tax? That latter-day commode my grandmother left me surely couldn't be worth that much? Unless it had served regal posteriors.

Then it might have had a tale to tell and command a royal price. Excuse the puns.

I certainly hadn't got eight thousand waiting for this bill. I would have to search hard to find eight thousand pence. I had no option but to tackle my antagonist head-on. It was eleven o'clock when I entered the tax office to keep my appointment. Its mere appearance gave me a feeling of despair. Dark corridors and large sprawling offices, filled with files and case histories of thousands of individuals like myself, filled me with a sense of foreboding.

This feeling was reinforced when I was shown into a large office and Mr Grabbit, sitting behind an enormous desk, resembled my mental image of Scrooge down to his stiff upturned collar and long finger-nails. I felt I was about to be interrogated, or worse, until I submitted to his demands.

"Aah, Mr Smith. So you have decided to pay up at last after all those letters you ignored."

"But I have only received one. This one. I'm---"

"Now Mr Smith, don't try to pull the wool over my eyes. I get hundreds like you. We know the tricks so don't try them." "But......."

"No buts about it. You have inherited your country seat now you must pay the tax." So it was my commode.

It must be worth a fortune if I owed that much tax. I excused myself without commitment and went straight home. It was only when I arrived that I realised I had achieved nothing. Mr Grabbit had dominated the discussion and I had succumbed to his authority. I rang my local antique dealer and asked him to come round and value my commode.

"There you are," I said, "its worth a fortune."

"That's what they all say," said the antique dealer, "Actually, it is early 19th century and only worth around two hundred and fifty pounds." Again I rushed for the brandy bottle, gulped another treble and just remembered to offer my guest a snort too.

"But they are charging me over eight thousand pounds inheritance tax on that thing." I said.

"There must be some mistake. They can't possibly assess for anything approaching eight hundred, let alone eight thousand pounds tax. I'll give you a written estimate if you like." I accepted, and paid him an agreed fee and he went on his way. I couldn't face Mr. Grabbit so I sat down and wrote him a letter explaining all I knew about my inheritance, and enclosing the written valuation from my local antique dealer. That was five months ago and I still haven't had a reply except an acknowledgement of receipt. Of course the seven days notice has turned into a court order, and I am expecting the bailiffs any minute to remove my life's possessions from right in front of me. I have become nervous, withdrawn and tend to shout at people that I meet.

Wait a minute; that was someone at the door. It's them, I know it's them, shall I answer it? Can they really take all I own? It isn't fair! What have I done to deserve all this? I'll open the door slightly, leaving the chain on. They can't enter that way. I can't see anyone. "Hello, who's there?" No answer. "Come on,

189

who's there?" Still no answer. I'll slide the chain back and open the door gently--------there is, no one there!

As I stepped back inside I saw a letter on my mat addressed to Mr R. Smith. The house number was thirteen, not three. Was this it then? Was there a second R. Smith at thirteen, and they got the address confused?

I ran round to number thirteen and there it was, R. Smith on the doorbell. My namesake listened to my tale of woe and then informed me that his country seat was a dilapidated old mansion in the far neck of the woods. He had donated it to the National Trust rather than pay a penny in death duties. He also said he had informed the tax office some eight months ago but had never had a reply. That's par for the course, I thought, this I wrote to the authority and haven't heard from them since. That was six months ago.

They didn't even apologise for the living hell they subjected me to for the cock-up in their addressing department. Beware of the Tax man. He often knows not what he does and cares even less.

From the early days of tax collection, where the peasants paid in kind or in the going currency, the groat, the Tax man has been looked upon as a villain by Us Folk. Although today he sits in an office he still relishes his sack-full of our groats.

Tax has to be collected but if we would only change to a negative tax system or as it is sometimes known, a credit tax system, we would need far fewer Civil Servants to administer it. This system removes the quaint practice of taking tax in one hand and going through an expensive system before returning it with the other. Other countries use it efficiently. Why can't we? Maybe it doesn't go further than the civil servants who stamp on any scheme that reduces their power or numbers.

IF IT DOESN'T MOVE TAX IT

For several decades the town planners have failed the motorist by not supplying adequate off street parking facilities near shopping centres and large office complexes.

In doing so they have created the situation we find in most towns throughout the country. If facilities are made available in the right places there is no excuse to park illegally. Where there is no such facility parking illegally is understandable. Towns like Staines can justly say there is no need to park illegally. Unfortunately their example is seldom matched.

Up till recently parking fines and fines for over-staying your time on parking meters have been at a reasonable level.

Now suddenly a government decision has been taken to clobber the poor motorist, Us poor mobile Folk, in a ruthless fashion.

First we saw a concentrated, privatised grab in London by licensed car lifters, who spirited our cars away to their lair where we had to pay enormous bribes to have them released. Naturally the companies were in business to make money so the cars lifted most regularly were the ones nearest the pound and in the wider streets that enabled fast access to lifting. This way they maximised their taking.

Did it solve the parking problem in London? Not a bit of it. It just frustrated motorists and blocked highways while they lifted the cars. Along with this absurdity they introduced car clamping in some areas. Did this deter the motorist or solve the parking problem? Not a bit of it. It managed to keep cars parked for an average of four times as long as they would have normally stayed and frustrated motorists who could not find a legal space within reasonable distance of their destination.

Both those options are, in my opinion, legalised theft.

Fresh from the success of boosting revenue the government saw a new way of boosting treasury funds by the worst state grab of them all. A fine system for all petty offences linked to earnings. This tax was not instigated by the home office, nor the department of the environment. Guess who did it? No, not the local authority. Did I hear you say the treasury? Right. Yes, with the skill of a surgeon they metered out the flexible fines according to means. This fine covered all petty offences and was cynically aimed at extracting extra money from the people least likely to complain, the silent majority of Us Folk that are generally at pains to abide by the law.

We saw one man fined seven hundred pounds for staying twenty minutes too long on a parking meter. Another was fined twelve hundred pounds for dropping litter and many other outrageous fines.

However the silent majority did not stay silent and the bad law had to be revised. The fact that it was a treasury attempt to fill their coffers from Us Folk was an assault on our hard earned and I might say depleting assets, while the real criminals were getting off with cautions for stealing and wilful damage.

Now we are hearing talk by politicians that we could be charged to use the motorways we have already paid to build.

Another state grab with an ill-founded argument behind it.

What we really need is a total re-think of our transport system and the use of the most ecological and economical forms of transport to cover long haul, interlinking transport and international travel for both goods and Us folk. Then lets put our money on the system and make it the envy of the World. I personally believe from this report we would get a borne again railway network; fast, efficient and cheap.

For their attempt to turn justice on its head I think this government should get the order of the "Sack."

THE VATMAN

He seeks us here, he seeks us there,
He seeks us almost everywhere,
Unless we're in heaven or in hell,
he'll tax our hearts and sound our knell.

From where did this hidden tax materialise? Hidden, because unless you have an official invoice you don't realise its presence. It materialised about the same time as decriminalisation and in preparation for our entry into Europe. A better name for it would be Europe tax." It is the price we pay to be a member of the European community. To be fair to Europe the market only gets a small percentage of the tax, between two to five percent depending on its yield. Some of it replaces import tax and purchase tax that went out of the window when we joined the EU. The EU became lovingly known as the 'Enormous ECU Con'. The rest of the tax goes into the ever greedy tax coffers, as usual.

Being based on sales it has two properties that dominate its usefulness to government. The first is that it is cheap to collect. Businesses collect it and pay it over to the customs and excise. They act unfairly as unpaid tax collectors with the additional dubious pleasure of having to pay it over to the customs and excise quarterly. Some would say it was free finance. Others might claim it was an uphill burden to collate before they were penalised. Furthermore it can be promoted as a wealth tax, as it is levied on sales, on the principle that the well-heeled buy more than the poor. This argument is always a good selling-point for the politician.

Against the tax is the uncertainty of its yield. It performs best in times of economic growth and worst in times of restraint. Government itself can hold back its yield by exercising a firm clamp on the economy. The point that is seldom mentioned by any commentator or even politician is the fact that it is a tax on already taxed earnings, just as poll tax or the hash up that replaces it. It is the tax man's second bite at the earnings of Us Folk. The tax is not choosy. It traps people on social security as well as millionaires.

From this we see the extraordinary double act of the tax man taking in one hand and giving back to the needy with the other. This is a clumsy and costly way to handle the financing of the unemployed.

The men behind the tax are the Customs and Excise. You might wonder what they have to do with taxation. Going back to the beginning you will see that VAT replaced import duty for goods coming from the EU countries. They just retained the collection rights of the new tax. Every business with a turnover exceeding forty two thousand per annum is required to register as a VAT collector. The customs retained the collection of import duties on all other countries outside the EU. We pay double taxes on goods from outside Europe. Ever felt ripped off?

By the time the tax man from the inland revenue and the VAT office, not to mention your local authorities, have finished with you they have spent between thirty to forty percent of your gross earnings. No wonder we are considered one of the highest taxed countries in the world. That is why us folk struggle to exist.

The Customs and Excise have become one of the prime movers in bankruptcy cases against the mountain of businesses going into receivership. Yet this problem has been caused by high interest rates and a government imposed recession for such a sustained time that business confidence has collapsed.

Never before has any government held a recessionist policy for so long; and why? The reason is that a previous chancellor sprung his clamp on the economy at the wrong time and released a bout of inflation, for election reasons no doubt and banks have forced their selfish ideas on the government for their own enrichment. For this major error the chancellor's reward was a directorship of a bank with a telephone number salary to go with it. Where is the justice in this world? Or is it payment for services rendered?

The customs and excise in the meantime have wasted no time in bankrupting companies at a record rate; many of whom were the product of Thatcherism. A very mixed period of blessings and sorrows. The vigour with which they pursue their target is legendary and frightening. They have more power than the police to search your office and home. They are known to be ruthless in their pursuit.

Yet most of these businesses have been the victim of political mis-judgement and banking greed. A combination that would defeat all but the strongest businesses today.

VAT'S RIDICULOUS

I still can't believe it has happened. Four months ago I was hard at work running my wholesale business with my assistant and with part time help from my wife. We were struggling, but like many other businesses in the current political climate, just keeping our heads above water.

It had meant long hours and a great sacrifice by my wife who also had to look after our children and cook for all of us. A thankless task that is always taken for granted. I remember that Friday as if it were yesterday. I'd just finished preparing a large order and entered the contents into the computer for invoicing. I was preparing to start work on my VAT return when the second mail arrived. The usual pile of bills, another two sets of tables from the inland revenue both conflicting with each other, and a typed envelope. Curious to find out its contents I opened it first.

I just couldn't believe what I saw. I had just recovered from a massive rates increase due to the local government reorganisation and the introduction of poll tax. This change made my business rates rocket from two thousand two hundred pounds per annum, to six thousand eight hundred pounds. This after we were told that it should not make much difference. A typical political blanket answer.

To achieve a substantial economy I had to part with my store man, and I was left with only my assistant and my overworked wife.

Well there in front of me was my second blow. My rent bill doubled. The shock was traumatic. I paced up and down in a daze wondering how I could overcome this latest bullet out of the sky; I began to feel dizzy. I sat down and my wife, who happened to be in the office at the time, brought me a glass of water out of concern.

I started to gasp for breath. At this point I knew that something was seriously wrong. My wife, deeply concerned, called for an ambulance, and then came to comfort me. The ambulance wasn't long in coming and after examining and preparing me they administered oxygen to relieve my breathing.

The outcome of this drama was that I had suffered quite a severe stroke. When the initial healing had taken place I was ordered to rest for three months at least, without the strain of work, to build up my resistance again. Reluctantly I had to agree. My wife, god bless her, did her best to keep our family, run the home and keep the business ticking over. She wouldn't let me near the office or even talk about the office problems. I was kept in the dark for my own good. As I said, I was about to prepare my VAT return when my sudden illness occurred. Well, the short of it was that my wife didn't know about the urgency of the VAT return and only became aware of it when she received the first reminder.

Then it all started to happen at once. By the time she had done the best she could and submitted our return we had received an assessment with a strong letter.

Then, out of the blue, the VAT office decided to send their inspector, Mr Blood, for a controlled visit. By this time my wife was at her wit's end; not knowing what she was meant to be doing. This visit by Mr Blood was followed by a letter accusing us of a serious mis-declaration and imposing a heavy penalty.

By this time my wife was beside herself with fear. She had explained the tragic situation to Mr Blood but either his deaf aid was not switched on or he totally ignored her plight. Anyway, they were claiming an extra ten thousand five hundred and sixty eight pounds and sixty four pence over the amount paid. A penalty of five-percent on the total bill was also included.

Desperate to know what to do she rang our accountant. He tried his best to delay the matter until my return, but today my wife came home in tears and spilt out the whole sorry story.

Apparently Mr Blood, armed with a walking possession order and accompanied by a bailiff, marched into our office at ten thirty this morning and sequestered our entire stock, office equipment and all. This took place two months and eight days into my illness.

My heart attack cost me my business. My wife will probably never forgive herself. This thanks to Mr Blood 'The Sucker' and his team of heartless Vatmen who totally ignore the code of the tax payer's charter.

This story, based on an actual case history, is a chilling reminder of how compassion is a word that the Tax Man has never heard. How it is the VAT office is allowed to ignore the code of the taxpayer's charter is beyond me. Us folk must make sure they take heed of this code always.

ROADS

Roads, in today's world, are the arteries to survival and prosperity. Love or hate roads and the vehicles that use them the whole logistics of modern life today would come to a grinding halt without them. Working in Colnbrook I am made aware of the early use of roads. I saw how villages, like Colnbrook, sprung up around what was not much more than a dirt track, to serve the stage coaches on their long journeys to and from Bath, and cities to the West. Today, as elsewhere, Colnbrook's roads are metalled to cope with today's traffic. Roads throughout the ages have developed to meet the never ceasing demand for better access. Hitler's greatest achievement was his network of Autobahns; inter-linking all parts of Germany on fast direct roads. Undertaken to ease unemployment in Germany, it was later appreciated as one of the essential ingredients to German recovery after the second world war.

Unlike Germany, Britain has had a very patchy record on road development and general transport planning. The cynics would sum it up as; too little' too late. Others would say that if freight had remained in the hands of the railway network, everything would have been all right.

The most obvious factor to anyone with a little knowledge and reasonable common sense is the lack of overall transport policy that is well planned and executed and that includes future expansion. As we move towards a united Europe it becomes more important to have such a strategic policy. Unfortunately we haven't. Our roads are in disrepair and out of date. The M25, the London orbital road, is frequently blocked from traffic overload. This road is a typical example of planner's madness. Before it was opened it was known that it would be overloaded and would require at least five lanes, instead of the three that were built. Its surface was breaking up in places before it went into service, and it lacked service facilities and rest areas essential for drivers to re-fuel or relax to overcome tiredness.

Our railways have not fared much better. They suffer from many years of neglect, inadequate stock replacement and a Ministerial attitude of planned decline. This was heralded by the Beecham report and orchestrated by governments since that time. It has been a policy of 'leave alone' that has produced the result; a sloppy passenger service and a declining freight business. Rail should be our best method of transport if only the government would do some overall strategic planning for all our transport requirements into the future. This must take account of expansion as well as changing requirements.

You can't just plan roads in isolation. All forms of transport; air, sea and rail must be included. It is at this point the problem arises. Different ministries are jealous to protect their territories. The ministry of transport plans our roads and rail network but other agencies become involved. The department of the environment has to approve road planning to make sure they meet their requirements. The British airport authorities control most of the air traffic in and out of the airports. They are now a privatised company.

The greatest problem with our planners is the time it takes from conception of the need for say a road to the date it goes into service. Apart from the time it takes to purchase the land required for road development so many other factors come into play. Not least the situation where a road plan is agreed in times of expansion: by the time it is ready to construct recession has taken over so its construction is shelved till the next expansion. This can mean delays of five to ten years or more and end up producing a road that is no longer adequate for traffic flow as in the case of the M25.

For a long time now we have been hearing about the European tunnel project. While France has built its side and completed its rail link, we have only just approved the route for the rail link. This service was meant to be ready by 1992. Our planners have let

us down again and it will cost us dearly. We will probably be late for breakfast, lunch and dinner in Europe if we aren't careful. Needless to say Us Folk will be the losers.

What is desperately needed now is an authority that can make decisions on its own to direct transport in all its aspects of operation.

That means reversing the trend to road transport. Get it back on the rails in a modern container led system that can cope with its workload, using modern methods to speed up handling, and private firms to hold down the cost. That means use the best solutions exposed by the lessons we have learned in the last fifty years. The knowledge and expertise are available.

We need a planned road system to meet the future demand from both the motorist's and freight service alike. Let's look at America and other advanced countries and learn from their mistakes as well as their successes. We must plan adequate roads both into and out of our cities and build off road parking.

When you buy a car with so much tax involved you expect to be able to use it for your shopping, as well as your pleasure trips. If the government want to encourage people to leave their cars behind they must offer free travel into the town centre as an incentive. Only positive steps like this will answer the problems of our roads for the future. If Munich can do it, so can we.

Imported from the misty Isle at no cost, is a whole army of pick axe carriers and shovel leaners whom single-handedly and methodically go about the serious work of digging up our roads and blocking our progress. Yes, These mystical émigrés from the bogfields over the water have a devastating effect on our good humoured, natural instinct and turn us into bad

tempered ill mannered louts by the end of a day's serious motoring.

THE HOLE

Well, it wasn't a hole really, more like a crater; as if some bomb had landed, buried itself in the road and exploded, leaving a crater about three feet by six feet and thirty inches deep in the middle. The only problem was that it was so positioned as to render my drive redundant. No car could get in or out unless of course they had caterpillar tracks like tanks. The extraordinary thing was we didn't hear a thing. It appeared overnight, and I found my entrance was blocked when attempting to go to work the next day.

Now when a hole like this appears it stands to reason someone must have made it. At least, that is the plausible reasoning. For the next three hours I attempted, in vain, to find a local agency that would accept responsibility: having checked their lists there was no road-works planned in Acacia Drive by any of them.

I was beginning to feel isolated. Where could I find the perpetrator of this cavity? I decided to go down to the town hall to enquire further into this restriction of my mobility but I had to walk as my exit was blocked. On arrival I asked to see the director of works. I was ushered into a purpose built office with all the modern toys for important men to play with in their working hours. However, it lacked a hole in the floor outside his office.

I thought I would make my point by saying how easily I found my way into his office without a hole blocking my way at the entrance. My sarcasm was wasted as he was not yet aware of my abcess, but it

made me feel better. For the next twenty minutes he patiently listened to my story and then tried his best to locate the phantom hole digger.

"It must have been an emergency," he said, "otherwise it would not have occurred at night." He tried hard but could not locate a candidate to blame for my imprisonment. After two hours he had to excuse himself as he was due at a council meeting, but promised to continue the search when he came back.

Resigned to my fate, I headed home. On the way I took a short cut down Acacia Avenue. Strolling down, still deep in thought, I almost fell into a hole identical to mine. I say 'mine'. Now that's a joke!

Looking around I saw it was outside number eight. I lived at number eight Acacia Drive. Was this a co-incidence?

I went up to the door of number eight and rang the bell. A lady in her forties answered it.

"Sorry to bother you, but can you tell me why the road has been dug up outside your house?"

"Yes dearie, I can. We smelt a terrible smell of gas late last night and reported it to the gas board. They have repaired it now but the contractors have yet to come and fill in the hole."

We were speaking when the contractor arrived.

"Excuse me," I said, "did you dig a hole in Acacia Drive similar to this last night?"

"Indeed we did sir," said the contractor, "you see sir, we mixed up the road names being as how it was dark sir. Don't you be worrying, we will have it filled in no time at all, after this hole, sir."

It didn't occur to him for one minute that I had been a prisoner in my own house, and lost a day's work for good measure!

You must have seen the project undertaken by your local council. Maybe a simple road widening scheme with a traffic light installation job at a T junction. A job the contractor would take two months at the most to complete. Not these guys. They can do much better than that; they make it last nine months. In the meantime the traffic is disrupted five times as long. Yes, they aren't on productivity bonus so there is no pressure on them to finish. The next job will be the same. You can always tell a council team from the contractors. They stand around talking most of the time or sit in their portable rest room playing cards. Well, they have to otherwise they couldn't make the job last as long.

Then there is the pre-occupation of digging up the roads for pipe laying or repair. Just recently a new road was built in my area, badly needed due to a heavy increase in industrial traffic. It included building a wider bridge and strengthening and broadening the road, building two roundabouts and installing a special drainage system for flooding problems. The job was completed on schedule. Within one month the pneumatic drills were at work at one end digging it up again.

Our planning is abysmal. Is it too much to expect the services that use our roads to join in the planning process? Elcctricity, water and telephone services could join in plans for so they can do the digging first?

Recently a new breed of digger has entered the field of play, the cable television man. He is paid by the foot of pipe, so he rushes the pipe down the road, leaving a dark uneven line where ever he goes and only surfacing it properly when complaints flood in. Yes, these bogland dwellers are an unpredictable brand. Just when you think you have recovered from the last onslaught to your hearing, they are at hand to deafen you with their air drills and bogland profanities.

onslaught to your hearing, they are at hand to deafen you with their air drills and bogland profanities.

Wouldn't it be eminently sensible to lay services to the sides of roads rather than under them as in so many cases, or is that too simple? All this leads me to believe there is somewhere, hidden away in a spy-proof bunker, an organisation dedicated to causing untold misery to motorists. Let us take a look inside such an organisation to appreciate how they might go about their daily work:

INSIDE THE INSTITUTE
FOR DELAYS

"Right gentlemen, this is your controller for the shift speaking. We have a very heavy work load today, and I don't want any errors to occur this shift, so pay attention, and that means you, Shamus. We don't want the exit traffic blocked on early morning rush hour.

Our purpose today will be a general slowing of the traffic flow. So with this in mind, Patrick, will you take your team to junction fifteen on the M25 and set up a two lane road-block in both directions? Traffic must be brought down to one lane only. Time of set up 08.00 hours and removal 10-00 hours. For you, Patrick, that is eight o'clock start and ten o'clock removal. That should serve a dual delay on the M25 and on the M4. Any questions?....... Good, then get to it. Now Sean, I want you and your team to simulate a repair on the East bound traffic into London on the elevated section of the M4 before junction two. This will effectively bring rush hour traffic down to one lane, as there is no hard shoulder on the elevated section. Set up time 07.00 and finish 11.00 hours.

Sean, please control your team this time. We don't want any promotional slogans for the IRA daubed on the crash rails in Day-Glo paint. Any questions?....... Right, on your way.

Liam, it's your team's turn to block the M1. I know you have waited a long time for this chance, so make the best of it. I want a two mile block between junction nine and junction eight on the South bound carriageway. You can give them some chicanes and cross-overs to contend with which might slow them down even further. Make sure you have an ample supply of cones. We don't want the fiasco we had the other week when the cars didn't know where to go because you spaced the cones too far apart. Bring the traffic down to one lane and block off the hard shoulder. The Setting up time is 06.00 hours finishing at 11.00 hours. Then move it all to the north bound side for 15.30 hours till 18.30 hours to trap the home goers.

Any questions?....... Right Liam get your team on the road, and I hope you don't meet any blocks to delay you getting there on time as you did last time! Shamus, It's your turn for the M11. They seem to be getting used to your blocks on this road. So let's have a change. How about a chemical spillage? That should give them something to talk about. It certainly slows them down when they see us in our white space suits. Maybe they think we come from the moon. Mix in a few total standstills while you hose down the road. Say twenty minute duration each time. 08.00 hours set up and finish 12.00 hours.

Target the South-bound traffic, then switch to the North-bound carriageway at 15.00 hours and hold till 18.00 hours. That should sort them out nicely. No cock ups this time Shamus. Remember to wear your masks. It looks far more convincing. Shaun, your team has the M20 today. We already have a lane closure near Dover due to road improvement. We want to hit it again before London. So take your team and channel the West bound traffic into a census. Set up time 09.00 hours, and finish 17.00 hours. This block should be between junction ten and junction nine and Shaun, please don't allow your men to ask for contributions to the IRA. It doesn't seem right at a census, does it?

Well, that covers us for today. There was a problem. We had a team shortage today to cover the M23 but I tipped off the police about a suspected heist at Gatwick and they are setting up a road block near the M25 so that's covered." Later the controller picked up his microphone and spoke to his teams;

"That should ease the traffic in London. Good hunting men. Let's stop them in their tracks. Now lets go shopping."

———————————

I wish someone would tell me who employs them. Is it a government conspiracy? ... or maybe it is a dastardly plot by the IRA to bring our nation to its heels!!

The local diggers are the ones we see daily on our journeying. We've all seen them. The gas board come in and dig up the road and then go away after half filling their trench. Then the water board has its probe, leaving another unsightly wound in the road. Hardly before they have finished, British Telecom is there with its team of road wreckers digging away. Then, when you think they have all finished, cable television send in their contractors to dig up the whole area again. They leave in their wake grooved roads and badly filled pavements that Us Folk have to complain about vigorously to ensure the job is done properly. Who, in the first place, allows them to abuse our roads and paths in such a manner?

I think Patrick summed it up for us all when asked why he had dug such a deep hole in the road. He just popped his head above the top of the cavity and said; "I don't rightly know sir. My foreman told me to dig a hole here sir, so that's what I'm after doing." Apparently his foreman was called away urgently and wasn't there to tell him when to stop. No co-ordination, poor supervision and a lack of shared information between the agencies that dig our roads make the inconvenience so much worse and prolongs the torture. It must also be said that the results are poorly inspected and leave badly filled repairs that can last for months into years before they are properly repaired. The question; Who supervises Patrick?, must be asked.

A VIRGIN HAS LANDED

Air transport is on the whole an efficient service with a long service record. Unfortunately, through the inevitable amalgamations and fast growth of the air services they have become managerial nightmares with gross over-manning. The challenge to this has brought a breath of fresh air to travel and has now landed at Heathrow from the outer airports in the shape of a Virgin. Branson, if he can save himself from the pickle British airways have schemed for him, could bring cheaper air travel to us all and break up the cartel.

British Airways should examine their record and try to compete, instead of the underhand manner in which they have been trying to harm his image. We need more Branson's and less over managed airlines. There is one down, Pan Am, but many yet to reform or follow them to the point of no return. The cartel must not, on any account, be allowed to succeed.

Modernising our transport system should be a top priority. It needs two main thrusts. First, a comprehensive study that recommends a strategic plan. Second, a concerted drive towards stock renewal. It amazes me how many buses are running on our roads polluting the atmosphere. If cars have to pass CO_2 tests, so should the multitude of public transport vehicles. You see far too many of them belching out black and white smoke while stuck behind them on the roads.

Plan from rail transport backwards and you can't go wrong. Rail should be used for long haul deliveries. Road transport used to interlink this service to its final destination. This should also apply from airport to rail to road and the same should apply to the docks who are already well advanced in the container system. Road transport should not be used as long haul only, for interlinking transport and final destinations. Containerisation, is the answer, even for small consignments in shared units, on the same basis as the daily delivery system developed by the road haulage contractors.

The railway could compete economically given the will and the investment. It could even solve our congested road problems and pollution risks with the right encouragement. As it is at the moment, the road situation can only get worse as will the pollution. We have been told by fuel companies and government releases that diesel fuel is clean, and the tax is kept low to show the acceptance of these facts. It is beginning to become apparent diesel fuel is not the clean fuel that we have been officially told it is by the government and the multi national oil giants. Four reports in America and at least two in this country showed concern over environmental effects of diesel fumes on the population with a positive link to certain particulates being the main cause of lung cancer. These reports have been suppressed in both countries; we can only presume because of the power of the oil lobbies.

If this is so it is an international fraud on the people of the world, that's Us Folk. We should demand that these reports, which have been commissioned as long ago as the mid-sixties, be released for public scrutiny for us to judge if our political masters have illegally withheld vital information directly related to our well being.

Lets bring back another age of the train and modernise our transport linking system. Richard Branson would be an ideal innovator to head such a move. Trains, buses and the underground should be reliably available for our personal transport needs.

Trains interlinking cities and buses, with the underground in the larger cities, reserved for local travel. If these services were efficient there would be no need to duplicate them. It is pleasing to see small buses being used on quieter routes rather than cancelling the service. This is important.

Also important, if we want to encourage our car drivers to leave their cars behind, is a free travel system to our city centres. This does not mean free transport regardless.

It could be linked to a car park courtesy ticket thus excluding others from using the free service. If we do all this we will have gone a long way to solving our road problems. Only then can the planners access the need for further road improvements.

Something must be done now before Us Folk come to a grinding halt.

BANKS

THE EXTORTIONIST

It was a bright sun-shiny day at last, after a long period of rain filled storms. It is amazing how a warm winter's day can turn your inner gloom to hope and expectancy. That was just how I felt as I prepared for the day's toil by downing a good breakfast.

In this mood the rattle of the letter box brought hope of something good descending on my mat, instead of the usual delivery of a gaggle of inflated bills, for the mediocre services that rule our lives.

Even as I inspected the only letter and realised it was from my bank, somehow my subconscious led me to believe it was good news. Maybe my overdraft had disappeared over night miraculously. I was soon to realise, Christmas had passed, and it was not miracle time.

The letter from my branch manager related to my overdraft. It stated my facility ceased when I closed my shop, and there were now a formal application and guarantee to sign. Could I pop in and sign them when I was passing? That seemed, on the face of it, quite reasonable, covering an oversight for them.

To put you in the picture so you fully understand the position, my business account used a five thousand pound overdraft facility while my shop was trading, quite enough to cover my needs. When my shop closed due to circumstances outside my control, the bank allowed me to continue the overdraft although I did not require the full facility.

This was allowed to continue without a new agreement for one and a half years. Then, when the new breed of charge rates were introduced by my bank to claw back more money from Us Folk they started to formalise the system. So not only would they get the high interest rates charged, around seventeen and a half percent but also the fat fees for the arrangements and facilities separately.

I was not advised of the new charge rates at anytime. It just happened. So for a simple reduction in overdraft, to a formal figure of one thousand pounds, I had to pay excessive charges on top of the overdraft. This involved a seventy pounds arrangement fee and a further sixty pounds for a legal guarantee arrangement, these charges to be renewed each year.

Needless to say, when I was fully informed about the charges I paid two thousand pounds into the account from savings and asked them to cancel the facility. I was told I could not as it had already gone through.

Well, it does not take a genius to calculate that the facility would have cost me around thirty-one percent if I had used it for a paltry overdraft of one thousand pounds. Yet they had a signed, personal guarantee for this figure. If you think that is bad; if, as a private customer I used a consolidated account to repay my overdraft with the same bank, it would have cost me in the region of sixty-five to sixty-nine percent of the loan.

I didn't use this type of account but it still cost me one hundred and thirty-five pounds for a facility I have not used and they refuse to refund the charges. Is it any wonder that thousands of customers, both private and business, are at their wit's end? Businesses, whose meagre profits are devoured by this monstrous usury, who because of this bank greed and the government led recession, are collapsing in their thousands. Private customers, whose financial problems, not of their fault,

are a product of failed government, turn in times of hardship to the banks for guidance and help. They receive instead treatment similar to the extortion of a back street money lender. It is usury. There is no other name for it.

Sometimes I wish we really could put our bank managers back in the cupboard. Don't you? God help the students that go over their loan facility. The facility the banks seduce them into opening. If banks can't restrain their greed, the government should legislate to stop them robbing Us Folk.

Banking is a minefield of hidden charges and I strongly suggest all us folk query every charge made by our banks. That's a sad state of affairs but it is true. I know. It happened to me. Is it any wonder Us Folk are fed up with banks? However, this is only the tip of the iceberg.

They charge between ten and fifteen pounds for a cheque that bounces, forty pounds for an interview with the bank manager, and so it goes on. Yet none of these services were considered chargeable before. If they used to cover these services without charge, they certainly can today with the higher interest rates to support them.

First, we are paying for the demise of industry, and in particular bad lending practice as highlighted in the Maxwell affair.

Second we are financing the huge losses incurred by the banks in the property market, again through bad judgement by banks.

Third and most despicable, we are re-couping the bank's huge debt loans to the third World. The debts that the top men in the banks knew would never be

219

honoured, but which certainly lubricates the way to the honours list for the same top men.

Recently an exposé showed how this practice is common in industry where payments to the Conservative party can be linked positively to industrial honours. This practice, where ever used, does nothing but nullify any meaning to the honours in Us Folk's minds and demeans the whole process.

It is quite clearly wrong the way they use the accounts of the vast majority of their clients, Us Folk, to refill their depleted coffers when they make bad loans to dubious sources. In any other field, except in the civil service, which protects its senior members from accountability, they would get the sack, and quite rightly so. They continue in the same old way without learning lessons. Some even get honoured, while Us poor Folk pick up the tab. It's got to stop.

The bank manager today, alas, is merely a rubber stamp for the faceless bankers from head office. He can, only ease the pain of your banking experience if head office agrees and he has the mind to help. He therefore cannot be blamed for a greedy banking system. He can however, report your feelings back to head office.

Make sure about the exact charge for everything, including a visit to your manager.

The attitude of banks has to change towards their customers. Availability of service, in relation to their opening hours, has remained the same for as long as I can remember. They have added some small changes, like Saturday opening for advice only in a limited number of banks, and of course that infernal hole in the wall machine. How many times have you been to a hole in the wall and found it is either out of order or out of money just when you relied on its service? How many of Us Folk had to take a taxi from bank to bank till we

found one in a generous mood, then realising you had to pay the taxi, you were forced to draw out double the intended amount?

How many of Us Folk have been cheated by this monster in the wall and found it impossible to get anyone to accept responsibility?

I suspect the bank's true charge for anyone that does not have a substantial credit, is excessively expensive and only tolerated because we do not know what to do. There is adequate competition if we look around. The building society and the post office are two for people in credit.

Another option is to go to a money lender these days to cover borrowing.

Banks have tried to establish other lucrative business in insurance, pensions, mortgages. They even dabble in the stock market, yet they try to give independent advice to their customers on all these fields. They can't do both because, I suspect, the advice side slants the business towards the other side. That usually turns out to be more costly than going to the specialist in that field. This makes a mockery of the independence of the advice. Don't be hooked by the solid stone walls of the bank. Get competitive quotations.

Highlighted by the crisis in the ERM, resulting in our withdrawal from this monster that has held our interest rates up so high for so long, was the speculation by the currency traders. Despicable was the only way to describe the part played by the big banks in the demise of our currency. One dealer was honest enough to publicly expose how many millions he had made that day for his firm. He was immediately sacked for this exposure. This practice is selling our currency short and should carry a penalty of one hundred percent tax. That would stop this tartar's practice that is both short

sighted, and to use an old word, treasonous. Yet it is practised by our banks.

The truth is, banks have far too much influence on government policy when they are only one element in a country's performance formula. To create success you have to have; The right products, at a competitive price, maintaining a good quality, and satisfactory availability.

Finance is only one part of this formula. You need inventiveness for the right products. A trained work force.

Quality control. Forward planning and finance. All of these are equally vital. Productions of good competitive products are in constant threat from government change of direction and bankers whims. As long as money men and governments rule, production of even our best competitive products will suffer. Eventually these will disappear, leaving finance with nothing to fuel.

Wake up bankers. Get wise Folks, or we will all go down the tubes.

DON'T BANK ON IT

I was, even though I say it myself, a successful farmer. I attributed my success to the excellent training and advice I received while at farming college. Unlike my father, who was from the old school of self-taught farmers who learned by their mistakes. I avoided most mistakes through my knowledge gained at college and being able to access my finances with near accurate results. I had managed my farm of two and a half thousand acres for five years. I had been able to treble my yields, by careful use of land and good management of my livestock. Indeed, my farm had the reputation of producing the highest yield of top quality milk in the county.

Times march on and the machinery manufacturers have a habit of producing bigger and better farm equipment, designed to save cost and all importantly, labour. Labour is a high cost in farming and saving in this field can finance the purchase of such equipment and show on top of this a good return for the investment.

I also knew if I purchased the latest equipment many smaller farmers, without my capacity, would hire us to do their work. It would cost them less than laying out capital or raising debts. So it was not hard for the local farm equipment salesman to convince me a package of tailor made equipment he could offer would give me maximum efficiency. I only had to convince the bank manager of the need for such a commitment.

Preparing a cost effective plan to cover the loan period, was a matter of course for me before I confronted my bank manager. It was quite a surprise when my manager called to see me, before I was half way through my costing exercise.

I was even more surprised when he approached the subject of a loan, and he virtually sold me the idea of borrowing a substantial amount to modernise my farm equipment. He didn't let up until we had a verbal agreement without the sight of my forward plan.

He even told me I could go ahead and order the equipment, as my land would stand as a more than adequate security.

This was a perfectly normal statement by a banker when negotiating a loan so I gave it little thought. I did however finish my forward plan more for my own sake but I presented the bank manager with a copy. I did this to prove to myself rather than the bank manager the viability of the intended purchase of nearly two hundred and fifty thousand pounds worth of equipment. The bank just seemed to want to satisfy my every need. I suppose I should have studied a reason for such a generous attitude.

Well, in the first two years my conservative estimates were surpassed, and a bonus business of rental was making a handsome return. It went half way to servicing the debt loan and halving the charge on my farming enterprise. So it could be said it was a good investment all round. However the next year proved disastrous. Half way through the EU decided that cereals were being over-priced, and as a result the support level was being lowered and farmers should reduce their yields.

The consequence was the value of farm land came tumbling down overreacting to the announcement, it seemed that no-one realised that land is adaptable to other crops or uses. My land value fell over night from two hundred and fifty pounds per acre, to fifty pounds per acre and consequently its power as collateral fell accordingly.

The bank wasted no time in accessing this situation. Within a week they were demanding repayment of the loan within one month. Where was I to find over one hundred thousand pounds in one short month?

The stupidity of this farce was that I was still making a healthy profit and this despite the cut backs required by the EU. I calculated I would still come out on top with a few alterations to my field rotation programme.

Armed with these figures I went to see my bank manager, but although he was most apologetic, he said the matter was out of his hands and was a head office decision. I asked to see the faceless man at head office that could bankrupt me without a fair hearing, but I was told this was impossible. I offered, finally, to add my house to the land to increase the asset but this was refused.

It is now six months since the episode I would rather forget. I lost my farm, all two thousand five hundred acres against my guarantee. I will be lucky to get any of it back when the bank has finally managed to sell the land. Worse still, I am in my house surrounded by my land that is a constant reminder to me of my ill fated loan, and of a bank that doesn't honour agreements.

Today I found out that the agricultural equipment salesman that put together my equipment deal is in the same Masonic lodge as my bank manager. I also learned that they frequently set up deals together and target the richer farmers with tempting offers.

The banks, through a short-sighted blanket policy decision, have bankrupted a successful business that was still showing a profit and excellent potential.

The land value would eventually rise again after the current crisis was allowed to run its course. Banks can't see further than their noses accept when it suits them. Meanwhile, hundreds of farmers like myself have been bankrupted for no understandable reason.

Bitter? Of course I'm bitter. I have lost everything except my house and that serves as a tormentor. The little money I have left now resides in a building society. I don't trust bankers anymore. When land is no longer a satisfactory security, what is?

A Bank?

INSURANCE

Insurance is a safety net in our lives to cushion Us Folk from the unexpected. It is a necessary evil, but is it fair?

Let's look at an insurance company using one of their favourite tricks to hold on to claim money for as long as it can, while it earns them interest.

BETTER LATE THAN NEVER.

January had been a particularly cold month bringing snow and freezing temperatures to upset our hopes for our financial prosperity. Long icicles hung from the roof gutters, resembling transparent swords ready to claim their passing victim whenever the thaw came.

I eventually arrived home that night after a tiring journey from my shop, caused by a combination of the appalling road conditions, and drivers with little sense upstairs in their brain department.

I was more than ready for a hot meal and a long hot soak in my bath and straight to bed. On closing my curtains I noticed that the windows were completely covered in white frost flowers, confirming my opinion that this weather was set to last for some time.

Eventually I climbed into my bed, warmed by my most luxurious possession, my electric blanket. At this point you are safely tucked up in your bed and gently warmed by its facilities. The toils and care of the day seem distant to you. Your long awaited satisfaction is complete, so it was on that night.

My rude awakening came at five minutes to three in the morning when my phone rang. Blurry eyed and half asleep I answered; The policeman on the other end apologised for awakening me but thought I should know that water was pouring out of my shop. How soon could I get there?

There is nothing like a shock to bring you to your senses. I raced to get dressed and collect torches, buckets, mops and of course my wellington boots and rushed to the scene of the disaster.

All sorts of terrible images went through my mind as I drove to London. On arrival my worst fears were confirmed. It was obvious the tank or the mains pipe to the tank in the loft had frozen, and in the late night thaw de-frosted and caused what only looked like devastation.

My first task was to get the main's water supply turned off but the pavement was still a mass of hard trodden snow and the turn off point nowhere to be seen.

I opened the door to the shop to be greeted by a torrent of cold water rushing to get out. The ceiling was half down and water cascaded down onto the shelving beneath. I knew then it was going to be a hard long night followed by a damp depressing day.

I went to the phone box and rang the water board emergency service, who promised to send a man urgently, but the voice added they were very busy. Amazing how they are always very busy when you are desperate. I decided to improvise a tool to shut off the water and after shovelling the snow away I found the cover, opened it and went to work on the valve. After several attempts I devised a way of turning it using a spanner and a pair of pliers thus reducing the flow to a trickle. For the first time the panic started to ebb.

Thank goodness I had my wellington boots with me as the floor was ankle deep in water. I went upstairs to the flat above and the ceiling in both the front and back rooms were also down. An ominous glow came from the lights where the water shorted the circuit.

Up in the loft I found the source of the leak. A burst main pipe leading into the tank that, although it was lagged, had frozen through the extreme cold of the last

231

two weeks. Thaw had come that night against all expectation.

All night and well into the morning I was bailing out the water and trying to rescue as much of the stock as possible.

The water board came at six-thirty to turn off the mains fully.

It was damp and cold in the shop but I didn't dare use any of the electrical fittings. The place looked as if a bomb had hit it.

By half way through the day the shop was useable and the shelves, though missing large sections of stock, ruined by the water, were at least tidy and dry.

In the following week an estimate to property and stock was prepared and submitted to the insurance company. Two weeks later an insurance inspector came in to examine our claim.

This was where I made my first big mistake. I should have employed a loss adjuster to make my case because I found after six months, stock that I considered unsoiled at the time, due to dampness had become soiled. A loss adjuster takes into account this and many other items that I omitted to include in my claim. He pays for himself handsomely. They say you have always got to do things twice in your life to do them correctly.

A further two weeks passed and I heard the insurance inspector had recommended his firm to accept my claim. Great, I thought. I can now restock my shop with replacements for the damaged goods. Wrong. For five and a half months after the inspector recommended the claim should be paid in full, the company played a cat and mouse game with me.

Each week I rang to find when I might expect settlement of my claim. At first they would say it was being processed. I don't know why? A cheque just has to be filled in and sent. Ten minutes work at the most. Once a claim has been agreed it should be a matter of minutes not months. Later they changed tactics and said the claim was with another office, so it went on week after week, excuse after excuse.

I decided this unacceptable situation needed action, so I took a leaf out of the suffragette's book. I rang the company again and told them I was on the way to their office and I would expect a cheque to be ready for collection. They began to make the usual, now familiar, string of excuses. They didn't have the paper work in the office but they would chase it up. This after five and a half months. I was furious.

I packed my case with sandwiches, drink and a pair of handcuffs with a secret release that I borrowed from my daughters magic set, and proceeded to their office.

On arriving I asked for the manager by name and was ushered into a sumptuous office. A bespectacled man in his late forties sat behind the desk. I stated my business and again a Tailor-made excuse emanated from his clone-like excuse exit.

Without warning I produced the handcuffs and clamped myself to his desk.

"Right," I said, "you've got me till you pay me."

A shocked excuse exit tried to utter some words but they were unintelligible. He left the room and within ten minutes appeared with my cheque, signed and dated.

"There you are, you can do it when faced with an unacceptable alternative." I said as I pressed the release lever on the magic handcuffs.

The clone-like excuse exit did not reply.

If we are one day late in paying our insurance premium they can claim we are not insured. If, however, they take months and sometimes years to settle a claim, we have no comeback. A bill of rights is required to address this and many other grievances experienced by us poor folk. Look at the debacle of Lloyds, the world renowned centre for insurance brokerage. It's gone through a bad patch in the last three years and some of its underwriters have been asked to pay out large amounts to cover claims. These claims have been for various reasons, one of which is the change of weather pattern as a result of global warming, caused by the greed of the developed countries, a large number of which are insured by Lloyds. In future Lloyds should penalise the big polluters to compensate for their changed risk, but current claims have to be met by the underwriters.

Most of the underwriters have, for years, gleaned fat returns for their membership and in return accepted liability for insurance cover. So when it comes time for them to put their hands deep into their pockets I can find no pity in my heart for their plight. I can however give them a word of advice. Don't commit yourself beyond a figure you can afford to lose and don't use your home as a collateral asset. They are in a gambling club, therefore they must expect to lose up to the value of their cover.

After all they also win big dividends each year.

We have all experienced the dubious pleasure afforded to us by a visit from the life insurance salesman. All salesmen are totally predictable. They first get their foot in the door. Then they spin a good yarn sprinkled with dubious humour. Finally for the kill, they offer you a closing bargain designed to make you decide with urgency to sign on the dotted line. Their foot in the door, in the main, is more subtle than most, as it is done by your mortgage broker, accountant, solicitor, bank or service you already use. They get an introduction fee for your business.

Have you noticed how depressed you get after a visit from your life plan man? He can make scarce tragedy seem common place, and fatal disease an everyday hazard. By the time you have listened to his patter it is surprising that anyone could resist his treaty to sign his life plan. His alone is inflation proofed and the best performer on the market.

If by any chance you have not succumbed by this time, his closer will have you rushing to put pen to paper when he says that at your next birthday it will cost you ten pounds more a month for the same cover.

Oh yes, they are taught how to worry you sick and then throw you a life line.

Be warned, some plans are better than others. Don't believe their statistics. They often have no relevance to your life plan. Compare offers and then decide even if it means listening to the same patter a few times. The salesman usually gets the best part of your first year's contribution for his success. Don't pity him. Always get competitive quotations: even on existing insurance when it goes up on renewal. This little story will tell you why.

A DEMAND TOO FAR.

It has long been the practice of my mortgage company to send its bills in smart white envelopes with windows. So that morning when one such envelope descended gracefully to my door mat, I was not surprised or even curious enough to open it until I returned in the evening. On opening it I expected to find the usual statement or advice relating to the change in mortgage rate.

236

I read it with an air of disinterest and nearly filed it as a statement, when I saw a figure they had entered for house insurance. I couldn't believe my eyes.

I knew it was index linked to building prices but the increase was grossly inflated. I read the enclosed letter that stated the index-linked value for rebuild had not risen this year, but the percentage coverage had been forced up by claims.

The insurance fourteen years ago when I bought my house was one hundred and four pounds per annum. The new bill fourteen years later was four hundred and fifty-six pounds, an increase on the previous year of thirty-eight percent.

Now I don't know about you, but I have found in the last few years it has become increasingly difficult to make ends meet, and increases of this nature are just unacceptable. I decided to ring my mortgage company office, as they handled the house insurance as a requirement to getting the mortgage in the first place. I was put through to the deputy manager and I asked her to explain why the insurance had increased by thirty-eight percent.

The reply was amazing, especially in its direct off hand manner. It was their considered requirement, and if I didn't like it I was at liberty to go elsewhere.

Not accepting the tone or implication of this argument I persisted, and stated quietly but firmly I was insured with them and as such required an understandable reason for such an increase. Again she repeated her arrogant message and again I insisted on a reasonable answer, only to be told the conversation was at an end. She put the phone down.

Well, I am not used to this sort of treatment, especially by someone who wants me to dig deep into my pocket. I decided to write to the managing director to get an explanation for the increase and a written letter of apology from the assistant manager.

Meanwhile I have tried a few other insurance companies and I have reduced the cost to two hundred and fifty-six pounds. A little over half of that demanded by my mortgage company.

Us Folk, on near static earnings, cannot be pushed into ever increasing overheads that take no account of our potential earnings. Over a period of fourteen years my insurance bill increased four hundred and fifty percent, that year alone thirty-eight percent. Where do they think we get these sort of resources to pay these inflationary demands? The cynical part about this case is for years the company had increased the insurance by use of the rise in the index linked re-build value.

When they found in the last year that they could not use the index linked rate to boost their input, they had to turn to the insurance rate per pound percentage to effect an input increase. This shows up as an increased demand rather than an increased coverage. It forced the true reason for the increase into the open: a fall in revenue that had to be counter-balanced. Surely they should cut their cloth according to income and not pass on their redundant capacity to be financed by their poor customers. Private business has to use this discipline and it's about time our public sector and the institutions did the same.

I am suspicious that the increases I experienced, and I am sure you did as well, are a result of the poor management of the insurance brokerage market. I am convinced that in our payments we are being billed for extra to ease the burden on the Lloyds names that underwrote the insurance. This is done so the insurance brokers remain in business and have their bad deals covered by Us poor Folk.

My final advice to all of Us Folk is to get competitive quotations when taking on any type of insurance and if a renewal increases without an explained reason, do the same.

There are good companies but they take some finding. Insurance is, after all, buying peace of mind. Therefore that is what we should aim to achieve.

EFFECTIVE COMMUNICATION

These are an example of extracts from accident claim forms received by an insurance company. I take no credit for its humour. This is all your own work folks!!

1   The accident was due to the other man narrowly missing me.

2   I collided with a stationary car coming in the opposite direction.

3   To avoid a collision, I ran into the other car.

4   There were plenty of lookers-on but no witnesses.

5   The water in my radiator accidentally froze at twelve midnight.

6   I was scraping my nearside on the bank when the accident happened.

7   After the accident a working gentleman offered to be an independent witness in my favour.

8   I collided with a stationary tree.

9   There was no damage done to the car as the gatepost will testify.

10   The accident was due to the road bending.

11   The witness gave his occupation as a gentleman, but it would be more correct to call him a garage proprietor.

12   I told the idiot what he was and drove off.

13   I remember nothing after passing the crown hotel until I came to and saw PC Brown.

14   A cow wandered into my car. I was afterwards informed the cow was half-witted.   (Must have mad cows decease!!)

15   A bull was standing by and a fly must have tickled him because he gored my car.

16   She suddenly saw me, lost her head, and we met. (Love at first sight.)

17   If the other driver had stopped a few yards behind himself, it would not have happened.

18   I bumped into the lamp-post which was obscured by human beings.

19   I crashed into a shop window and sustained injuries to my wife.

20   I blew my horn but it would not work as it was stolen.

21   I consider neither vehicle was to blame, but if either was to blame it was the other one.

22   The car in front stopped suddenly and I crashed into it. (Must have been a Toyota.)

23   Coming home I drove into the wrong house and collided with a tree I haven't got.

24   I looked for the sign but the more I looked the more I couldn't find it.

25   Ice on the road applied the brakes causing a skid.

26   I heard the horn blow and was struck violently in the back, evidently a lady was trying to pass me.

27   A pedestrian hit and went under my car.

28   I left my Mini outside, but when I came out later, there, to my amazement, was Rolls Royce. (If you wait long enough everything grows on you.)

29 One wheel went into a ditch. My foot jumped from brake to accelerator, leapt across the road and hit a tree.

30 Three women were all talking. When one stepped back and one stepped forward I had to have an accident.

31 I misjudged a lady crossing the street. (It must have been Dolly Parton.)

32 I thought the side window was down but it was up as I found out when I put my hand through it.

33 On entering Wales, I blew my horn at the left hand corner.

34 I knocked over a man. He admitted it was his fault as he had been knocked down before.

Keep them rolling and I will publish a book of your master sayings. The humour is great, congratulations.

THE LEGAL PROFESSION

SOLICITORS

Solicitors, you would have thought, as one of the oldest professions, could have got their act together by now and delivered their knowledge in understandable English. Not a bit of it. When have you seen a simple to read legal document? They have developed their skills so well that the average person knows little of what they are describing, this way they need another solicitor to translate their legal dialogue, thus creating work for another solicitor. That has to be the prime reason they word it in this way.

Most of the more common legal documents can be pre-planned and stored on a computer and be called up as required. This action makes the need for a solicitor redundant, but as this would reduce the work load by over half, and leave a string of unemployed solicitors, they bye-pass modern technology to maintain the status quo.

Instead they baffle us with long dialogue to say simple things, and charge us telephone numbers for their services. Yes, Us Folk get horrendous bills for their fees. Their bills are far out of proportion to any work they have done. When we query their charges they slide into their other language of the legal jungle to confuse Us simple Folk, so we usually pay up rather than take more of their jungle talk. We pay large bills for something an average intelligent human being could have written down in plain English in a fraction of the time, and for a far more reasonable fee.

A purposely simple example of this language can be taken from any legal document, for example a company memorandum and articles of association, page two section E;

To purchase or by other means acquire and protect, prolong, extend and renew whether in the United Kingdom or elsewhere any copyrights, patents, patent rights, trade marks, designs, rights of production or other rights, brevets d'invention and licences which may appear likely to be advantageous or useful to the company and to use and to turn to account and to manufacture under or grant licences or privileges in respect of the same and to spend money in experimenting upon and testing and in improving or seeking to improve any patents, inventions or rights which the company may acquire or propose to require.

What a mouth full. My computer's grammar check nearly blew a fuse when it hit this passage. Section E means in simple language;

The company has the right to purchase or acquire, extend or renew world-wide the following; copyrights, patents, trade marks, designs, rights of production, rights of publication, brevet d'invention and licences useful to the company and improve on their design. It also has the right to licence same.

Doesn't this put the same thing in a much more understandable form and save our forest assets at the same time? Remember I chose a relatively simple example. Think of the contribution to the environment simple plain English on these documents could achieve.

This is a very good reason why Us Folk should avoid the use of solicitors if we possibly can. You can now do house conveyancing and will preparation, along with a host of other simple work, at a fraction of the cost incurred through a solicitor. The legal profession has priced itself out of reach of Us average Folk, and therefore justice in its more complicated area's is an affordable luxury of the very rich or the very poor who can claim legal aid and get an over heated service. This, I hasten to add, is not the fault of the generous solicitors who forgo their potential gold mines to serve in this field, but the consequence of demand and inadequate funding.

It is the people in the middle of our society that are left without an affordable system. They fail the means test for legal aid but are unable to afford the high legal costs of any litigation.

If we are going to make legal representation available to all that require it, something has to be done to sharpen up the court practices. Solicitors and barristers waste half their life away waiting for their case to be heard and have to charge their clients accordingly.

I have always made it a practice to get a written quotation for all legal work since the episode I once endured while buying a house. From this moment I lost total regard for the legal profession due to the nightmare of events that unfolded.

THE INCOMPETENT

What do they say? Buying a house is the biggest decision in your life. Well, I would add to that; the greatest problem filled drama you ever participated in.

It all started when my wife and I decided to move further out of London to be nearer to the countryside but remain in easy reaching distance of the city. We started to look in the Berkshire area and visited many potential properties, none of which reached our expectation until, we were sent details of a house just outside Windsor. We thought it looked promising but estate agents usually dress up an old rooster to look like a spring chicken so we reserved our judgement.

Well, it's an extraordinary thing, but as soon as I put foot in this house I knew it was home. We prepared for the big event by putting our house up on the market, and started to search for a mortgage company to accept our request for a small mortgage on our new found treasure. Well, that proved to be elusive. Our old company did not want to know and it proved impossible to get a straight mortgage anywhere. As it was my accountant who insisted we move to re-start a mortgage, I decided to approach him to see if he had any suggestions.

It turned out he knew a mortgage consultant whom he recommended and put him in touch with us. It seemed we wanted to move at the wrong time as there was the worst famine of mortgages he had ever known. I remember at the time I thought he was only saying that to sell us his services but later on I found it was true.

He said he would try but in the present circumstances he couldn't promise anything. However, eventually he came up trumps and found a company that made me an offer. His condition was that I had to take out a life policy that I did not need, to cover his commission. In the circumstances that seemed reasonable,, and life insurance is always a worthwhile investment.

What I found disturbing was that he insisted I used a solicitor he knew to handle the conveyancing. I only found out when it was all over that the solicitor held the introduction to the mortgage. At this point the most difficult part of the transaction should have been settled. Little was I to know what was round the corner.

I showed my house to over ten potential buyers and a married couple showed real interest. They decided to proceed as indeed I had done with my potential purchase. I remember thinking at this point everything seemed to fit together like a jigsaw. Little did I know jigsaw bits go missing.

So it was on that day, when an off white envelope with a typed address landed on my front door mat, I knew it was from my solicitor. When I opened it I found a request for information required by the mortgage company. I made it a practice to reply to these requests by return and on my way to work I put the answer in the post to my solicitor.

About two months later the seller of the house I was purchasing and the buyer of my house began to request a contract signing date. I requested my solicitor to find out when this could be arranged. As I did not get a satisfactory answer from my solicitor, I rang the company that offered the mortgage, to find that the information they had requested over two months ago had not been passed on to them. They had assumed the mortgage was no longer required and they had passed

the money on to another applicant. That was it. No money. My solicitor had not passed on the information and had consequently lost me a mortgage facility that had cost me a life insurance to obtain.

I was furious. After this point I had to double check everything the solicitor did to make sure it was done properly. The mortgage broker found another mortgage but I had to ensure the house through the mortgage company instead of using my existing policy as cover.

In the meantime the owner of the house I was purchasing began to think I was messing him around, and gave me an ultimatum threatening to put his house back on the market. Little did he know how I was struggling against the odds to comply with his wishes. When we got over several other small delays we set a date to sign the contracts on both deals on the same day. This complete, I thought nothing else could go wrong. I was wrong. A day after the contract signing my house purchaser came to see me, to tell me he must have been mad to sign the contract. He was splitting up with his wife and he must call the deal off. I was sorry for him, but I could only think of what this would do to the purchase of my house. So I simply told him it would cost him more to pull out at this stage than to proceed. It must have had the desired effect as three days later he decided to proceed. Those three days were the longest in my life. Despite all the difficulties, completion was only one week late from the original target.

Instead of the solicitor taking the strain of the purchase I had virtually done his job. On completion I was amazed to receive a bill for his services amounting to twelve hundred pounds, not including stamp duties and other sale costs. This bill followed his failure to do his job properly, thus endangering my purchase. I tried to get his bill taxed by the law society who, I was told, officiated over complaints between solicitors and clients. All they did was to protect this solicitor from my

247

justified complaints about his conduct. I also found it was impossible to find another solicitor who would take my case up against this solicitor.

As a solicitor deducts his fees before passing back the balance of deals he cannot lose. Us poor Folk always end up the losers and sometimes have our dreams shattered by the professional incompetent. Avoid solicitors if you possibly can.

A prostitute and a solicitor both solicit for business. I wonder which is the honest solicitor.

BARRISTERS.

The Barrister belongs to a lodge. He wears a powder-dusted wig with a long black gown. No, this is not speech day at school but barristers at work. They are your last ditch stand between justice and whatever alternative. With the ease of a maestro they will flit through the litigation of time, using this case or that president to prove their case. The best are priced out of reach for Us poor Folk. Only the state or the rich can afford their fees. The balance present pot luck. All too often you get an incompetent that is known to judges and the bench alike for his ability to deliver the wrong ill prepared oratory about some other case. This will go on until the judge stops him in his tracks and advises him to have an early night before court proceedings.

Normally your solicitor chooses the lodge and the lodge allocates their advocate.

THE ORIGIN OF THE LAWYER

A girl rushes into a doctor's office in some state of confusion;

"Doctor, doctor, I've got to know if I can get pregnant after anal sex?"

"Of course you can dear, where do you think Lawyers come from?"

WARNING. Litigation in court can seriously damage your wealth.

COURTS

The court system is so badly organised that the people who should be willing witnesses, are being discouraged from coming forward with their evidence through delay, vague scheduling and problems of postponement. No one can afford to be repeatedly re-called to give evidence because of the bad court planning, and therefore they are reluctant to come forward in the first place. Because of this they could easily cause a miscarriage of justice. The system is far from perfect, and wrong decisions are made every day for lack of evidence or bad representation.

Justice is dependent on good representation and truthful evidence. If you have ever been in court, the first thing you realise is that it is totally impossible to follow the proceedings until the barrister addresses the jury. While speaking to the judge he uses an alien

language referring to previous cases and presidents to further his case. It is all a matter of reference that he should have looked up beforehand but which the judge is meant to recall. It is therefore impossible to hazard a guess as to which way the judge is thinking, except by his comments.

Once again the system is designed to exclude us simple folk from understanding the procedures but requires us to accept the consequence of the decision whether right or wrong. On the law of averages they must get it right some of the time. What is so worrying is that the average works the other way too.

The legal system is far from perfect. Quality representation should be available to all at an affordable price. The courts should organise their work-load in a more professional manner.

Justice is, after all, the scales that protect our society. It is a delicate balance that requires adjustment from time to time.

JUDGES

Judges are like the elders of an Indian tribe. Through their wide knowledge and long experience of the legal system, they have developed an understanding that allows them to guide juries on the correctness of the legal arguments of the case and reduce the warring factions to its legal obligations. Good judges can sway juries. They also have to award sentences relating to the jury's decision. It is in the judge's power to dismiss a case if he considers there has been a miscarriage of justice.

To give a controversial but never-the-less a good example, Judge Pickles, who is considered a problem judge through the record of his judgements and public

statements, has made a very interesting video of his case for the legalisation of drugs: a very emotive subject. His in-depth study of this field can only be admired however you feel about the conclusion. He actually made the effort to research his subject. This gave me confidence in his judgements.

It is as well to acknowledge that judges are human beings. They can only react to the evidence before them and guide the jungle of evidence into a channel of law. They, themselves, sometimes get brain-washed by the proceedings before them.

I remember talking to a lady of the streets about her clients. She specialised in correction and the interesting statistic was that most of her clients were judges and barristers who required to be dominated. It seemed they wished to be on the receiving end of punishment.

I am sure Freud would have something to say on this matter. We live in a strange world where the mind can be influenced by what we are and what we do.

JURIES

That's Us Folks. How the hell can we be sure of our decision amongst all this hype? Past prejudices must lead us.

Court hype only confuses us. Result: is it justice?

ESTATE AGENTS

To help you understand the language of the estate agent I have listed some of the more important expressions embodied in their sales sheets so you can understand there real meaning.

"In a sought after position."

Meaning; We have tried every other way of selling it and this is our last shot.

"Secluded position."

Meaning; No one else was mad enough to build another house in this god forsaken neck of the woods.

"Affording a spectacular view over farm land. "Meaning; The field at the bottom of the garden is inhabited by a bull where he performs his mating ritual.

"Semi-detached."

Meaning; Some cheapskate builder decided to save on material and build two houses joined together.

"Detached."

Meaning; Its on its own. Just! Without support.

"Standing in its own grounds."

Meaning; Nothing. Every house does. However the limit of those grounds is in your interest to establish.

"Landscaped garden."

Meaning; Someone dug some beds and put some plants in them.

"The lawn falls away to a shrubbery at the bottom of the garden."

Meaning; The house on the hill is a prime candidate for subsidence. The shrubbery was planted to stop the soil movement. Too little, too late.

"A four bedroomed house with two double and two single bedrooms.

Meaning; A house with two bedrooms and two further rooms with a bed filling each.

"Well proportioned."

Meaning; The brick-layer got the count right for a change.

"Situated in a quiet Cul-de-sac."

Meaning; Situated in a quiet Cul-de-sac next to a noisy main road.

"Terraced house."

Meaning; A run of houses holding each other up.

"Close to local facilities."

Meaning; The shops are fifteen minutes away. (By car.)

"--and within easy reaching distance of London.

Meaning; They have built a motorway past the house but the junction is within easy reaching distance. Ten miles away.

"Bargain of the week."

Meaning; We've tried in vain to sell this dog.

"New instruction."

Meaning; Only came on the books this year.

"Reduced for quick sale."

Meaning; We over priced this house. The sale is now urgent.

"Two bedroomed town house."

Meaning; A compartment matchbox.

"Luxury fitted bathroom and toilet suite."

Meaning; A room ten by six with a bath, wash basin and toilet shoe-horned into it.

"Adequate toilet facilities."

Meaning; An outside shed with a thunder box in it.

"Decor in need of attention."

Meaning; Wallpaper falling off damp walls. Plaster board bulging. Paintwork flaking. Woodwork rotting.

"Modern kitchen.,"

Meaning; They took out the old Aga and replaced it with an electric cooker and surrounded it with twenty-five year old kitchen units bought in a garage sale.

"Modern fitted kitchen."

Meaning; How could they have such bad taste?

"Outside finish guaranteed for ten years."

Meaning; By the time it goes wrong the company will have gone into liquidation.

"Large cloakroom off the hall."

Meaning; A cupboard under the stairs which you bang your head on every time you get your coat out.

"Large dining/living room area."

Meaning; You will be lucky to get your existing furniture into it.

"Well sought after area."

Meaning; Every local thief has had a go down that road.

"Easily maintained garden."

Meaning; It has been concreted over and flower boxes scattered around.

"We have a Mr. Potter very interested in this property."

Meaning; You are the first sucker to show interest in the last nine months.

"Mr. Potter is about to put down a deposit."

Meaning; "We are desperate to close a deal with you."

"Our client might accept an offer."

Meaning; The owner is desperate to sell and will accept an offer that will satisfy his mortgage company.

"My client might consider leaving his carpets and curtains."

Meaning; The carpets and curtains are worthless.

"The offer includes fittings and fixtures."

Meaning; My client will unscrew everything that is moveable and remove the light bulbs when he goes.

This gives you a gauge to judge each statement on its merit. At the end of the sales sheet on the house specification they run a disclaimer which virtually says that their sales patter is a lot of hot air and the measurements are not accurate. So what pray do they do for their large fee?

Would you bother to look at a house that was honestly portrayed, as a two bedroomed house with two further small rooms that would take a bed at a pinch?

Or perhaps a house that had cracks on the outside wall that could be due to subsidence. Hype is our way of selling and therefore this guide should help Us Folk to see through their flannel and examine the practical possibilities of the property. I hope so.

ACCOUNTANTS

An accountant is the person between Us Folk and the inland revenue that attempts to save us valuable sums of money by treading the grey path between tax avoidance and tax evasion. You might say he is a go-between that uses skill and tax loop holes to save our money from the greedy clutches of the devil tax man. The better he is at his job the more he is likely to charge you. What you must decide is whether you end up saving money. This is something many people fail to calculate. Remember it can leave you no better off.

So why do we bother? Perhaps the answer lies in our dreaded fear of the tax man, those monsters of penalising power administered so often on a whim.

Like all professions there are the good, the bad and the indifferent. To choose your accountant to fight your corner ask around. Personal recommendation is usually the best lead to the right person. Good ones don't come cheap. Cheap ones can prove very expensive.

Once you find a good one he will take over all your tax problems, including your personal returns. Do find the time to make and file a copy of everything you send to the revenue. They love to catch you out in a lie from a past form. If you slip up and give conflicting information to a previous form the vultures at the revenue will devour you. Its like a box of candies to them.

A good accountant is like a fox. He will painstakingly search through your accounts and juggle with the figures to avoid as much tax as he can by hiding it within the legal boundaries set by the revenue.

His sly cunning leads his assailant (the revenue) up blind paths and down dead ends in an attempt to head him off the scent. He will gain much pleasure from his chess game with the revenue inspector, showing no hurry to complete his kill till he has tired his assailant to the point of submission.

Unfortunately the revenue is now employing the top achievers from university, and tempting them into their midst with fat performance bonuses directly attributed to the tax gained, and are sometimes more than a match for our sly fox. It can therefore develop into a battle of the giants, forgetting the poor taxpayer, one of Us Folk, is the subject of their battle of pride and we can easily end up the loser.

Once the revenue gets his claws into you he will probably hound you for the rest of your natural. So beware of clever accountants with an oversized ego. They can condemn you to purgatory for a very long time.

It all boils down to the equation that if you get two figures they can be presented in many different ways. No wonder the same statistics can be so widely interpreted by politicians. No wonder that when you get ten economists in a room you get ten opinions on a solution to a problem. How are Us simple Folk meant to judge which course of action is best?

As a footnote to accountants I give you a few corporate sayings that could well land the user in the hands of his solicitor.

"The company assets have fallen in the fiscal year and action has been taken to remedy the situation."

Meaning: "Unfortunately we have frittered away the company securities and have done our best to hide our extravagances."

"The company pension funds are safely invested."

Meaning: "We have found a way round the law to get our hands on your pension money." (Big Bad Maxwell?)

"We're looking into ways of boosting the company funds."

Meaning: "We have found a way of putting your pension funds on a roller."

"We tried to tempt our main competitor into an amalgamation."

Meaning: "We've sent in a company spy to enable us to blackmail our main competitor into an amalgamation."

"At no time were any corporate changes discussed outside the boardroom."

Meaning: Someone inside decided to make a killing or told a friend who told a friend."

PILOTS

We all have our own romantic idea of an air pilot. My personal recollections were formed in my youth by those absorbing thrillers by W.E. Jones covering the intrepid adventures of Biggles and his world crusade against the criminal fraternity. He portrayed an image of a modern musketeer using the aeroplane instead of a horse to propel him to his adventures. His character was that of a daring pilot that was as good with a pistol as he was with his propelled transport. A man's man; a comrade to his friends and an inspiration to his team. He always gave his best when under pressure or in danger.

Pilots today have an impossible image to live up to, especially when Biggles, a fictional character, was followed by our brave boys from the battle of Britain and the bomber pilots from the second world war. A few names come to mind such as Sir Leonard Cheshire VC, Bomber Harris, and of course the remarkable Squadron leader Douglas Bader, romanticised by the actor Kenneth Moore in "Reach for the Sky's." However Douglas Bader, through his behaviour, gave a very real picture into the character that is essential in a pilot even in today's armchair flying.

Romantically he was a hero, a role model of courage for all to attain, but the truth was somewhat different. He lost his legs while disobeying clear rules laid down by the RAF to protect pilots from the accident that occurred. He was showing off in front of his fellow pilots.

It was this dare devil attitude, coupled with their arrogant behaviour, that saw them through what must have been the unbearable tension and distinct possibility that they might be the next to go missing in action.

Bader's arrogant personality saw him through the probability of death after his accident, in a way to prove the doctor wrong when he over-heard him comment to a nurse that he was dying.

It was this same arrogance that lead him to believe that he could escape from the security prison of Colditz; hitherto described as an impossibility. For a man without legs, it would most certainly be described as an impossibility, as the German commander had removed his artificial legs due to a previous attempt it was almost impossible. It required an act of complete defiance displaying very special qualities. Perhaps the moment creates the opportunity to show qualities, but the individual is left to perform.

After his accident his doctors said he would never walk again. He did. The German command said he could not escape. It was another challenge he met and defeated. In peace time he had another battle to fight. His pilot's licence was suspended, due to his disability. So he had to fight to regain it which meant making the authorities change their conditions to suit his handicap. He climbed this mountain too and reached the top.

His second peacetime ambition was to play golf. That for a man without legs seemed impossible, but with help from that amazing hospital at Roehampton he attained his goal, even though he fell over each time he hit the ball hard.

So where does this leave the modern pilot in this age of technology and achievement? He is of course, and has to be, highly trained. His ability must cover all the possible things that might go wrong or fail on his flying computer. Having said that, the planes today are almost self-flying, therefore checking the correct flight path is his main occupation. It must be a boring job, requiring a very different man from our erst-while heroes of time gone bye.

So what is the character of our air bus driver? Who better than to ask than his flying companions, the air hostesses.

Would it surprise you to know that they all seem to say, as if in unison, pilots are 'Nigels', that consider themselves the bees knees, walk around in what used to be called brothel creepers (very thick soled shoes), and dress abominably?

Socially they can't dance as they have no rhythm. They follow their self-centred hobbies like fanatical youths, especially if it is to do with aeroplanes, and for such well travelled people they have very limited knowledge. It is as if all the brain power is channelled into their work and number one hobby, flying.

Their most frequented social gathering place is in the pub, or club, and a surprising piece of statistic that was divulged to me, air pilots have the dubious honour to be the largest group of professionals attending alcohol dependency clinics in America.

Well after all that I wouldn't blame you for cancelling your flight but the other statistic is that flying is the safest form of travel, and due to its speed, the most convenient.

After all you can get killed crossing the road.

A FLIGHT OF FANCY

Nigel, for that was his name, was an established pilot with twenty-five years experience behind him. Married, with two children, he managed to accumulate a considerable liquid wealth in his years as a high earner. So when his airline asked for volunteers for early retirement due to the world wide reduction in flight slots, he saw an opportunity to retire early. Through generous retirement terms he would only lose twenty percent of his salary and it would give him the freedom we all look forward to in retirement. There was one snag. He had been living a double life for the past ten years. He had a lover, Helga, in Germany, with whom he had spent Tuesday evening through to Thursday on a regular basis.

At this point he could hardly tell his wife about his illicit liaison but it had become a habit he could not just forget. He resolved to continue his double life by hiding from his wife his decision to retire and continue as if he was still on his flight schedule every week.

As he received a ninety percent discount on flights, it was like taking the train on a medium journey, and should not affect his accumulated wealth and therefore show on his accounts should the wife inadvertently see them. It was, as far as he could see, a fool proof deception.

As time went by his confidence grew. Early on Tuesday morning he would dress in his pilot's uniform and say good bye to his wife as usual. Then, on the way to his flight he would change back into his casual clothes and take his flight to Hamburg.

Then, strangely, he would change back into his pilot's uniform because Helga adored uniforms. It turned her on! So he completed his circle of deceit by leaving his lust nest on Thursday for his flight home.

This worked like clockwork for three years, three months and three weeks but as the saying goes, all things must come to an end, and this double life certainly did just that. It all went wrong when his wife, on the Thursday of the fourth week wanted to make sure he received a message before returning from the airport. So she rang the flight desk to leave a message for him about their evening arrangements.

To her utter astonishment she was told he retired over three years ago. After swallowing the implications she decided to hear his lies once more before informing him of her knowledge.

When he arrived home she asked him, as usual, "How was your flight?"

"Oh, boring as usual. We had to wait twenty minutes over Heathrow before landing."

This was her moment of revenge and she intended to make the most of it.

"You deceitful liar. Get out of your uniform, you are retired. Get out of my house and get out of my life."

Silly Nigel lost his wife, his home and ninety percent of his liquid wealth for his flight of fancy. He could no longer afford his trips abroad, so he lost everything.

EXPERTS

Experts hide behind many names and guises that indicate their qualifications are the ones we should hire, but as Shakespeare said "What is there in a name?" As always Shakespeare hits the nail on the head and proves his thinking is timeless. He indeed, was a true expert.

So how do Us Folk protect ourselves from hiring an unqualified expert we need, who turns out to be a hyped up cowboy? That can be quite daunting as the reason that we require their services in the first place is that we do not have the knowledge to do the job. How then can we be sure they possess that expertise?

It is generally no good checking with professional bodies, because even if they are a kosher professional association and not just a cowboy outfit as so many are, they are paid by the member and therefore their first loyalty is to that member. This is particularly true of the law society, who you might think take up complaints against solicitors. Not a bit of it, they seem to try and shield any incompetence by their members from being taxed for their mistakes.

The building trade has all sorts of rogue associations and guilds supporting the cowboy element of the trade. When you realise that the only qualification required to join some of these pretend expert organisations is a fat fee for sham respectability: you realise it is a useless pretence of qualification. Great care should be taken before committing yourself to using a member of such a guild or federation. The best advice I can give you is to employ specialists by recommendation where ever possible.

I always remember such a federation representing locksmiths, calling at my shop to enrol, me in their scheme. I cut domestic and car keys. The representative told me the numerous benefits of joining their trade federation. When I asked him how I could qualify to join his federation he looked at me in amazement and said; "Hand over your cheque for seventy-five pounds and you're qualified. That sums up how careful you have to be in this age of hype.

A MASTER DISASTER

Buying a house is usually one of the high moments in your life. Having finally overcome all the hurdles along the way, (see solicitors) which can be daunting, you at last own your own house so it is totally natural to want to make alterations to suit your family needs. Well I don't know about you but my limit is decoration. I am not into structural alterations, so my first task was to find an expert builder to carry out alterations to the bathroom area and to build a shower downstairs.

When I first took possession of the house, I hired a floor sanding machine and sanded all the downstairs rooms, finishing them off with an epoxy resin for a hard finish. We did this job first as it was excessively dusty and we wanted it out of the way before we moved our furniture in. We knew the building work would also be dirty but more localised.

The time came to select builders, and I asked for quotes from three local builders, and one from London I knew from my shop. They all came with their quotes and left except one who showed us an album of his completed work and went through it with us. I must say, although he was pushy, I was impressed and we

decided to hire him to do the work. What finally decided me to hire him was the fact he was a member of A Guild of Master Builders. I was seduced by a title that I thought should mean something.

Well, number one disaster happened on the first day. He turned up around eleven-thirty having told us he liked to start early, unloaded his tools, and started his demolition work. We prepared coffee for him and his mate and found him wandering round the downstairs rooms inspecting our work on the floors.

We could trace exactly where he had been as he was wearing boots with metal studs in them. A trail of holes showed the route he took through the rooms. I blew a fuse.

We didn't see him for two days after that. He made pathetic excuses about not having the right materials to do the job but he made no effort to get them. When he did eventually turn up he came half way through the afternoon managing just two hours work. When pressed we established he was doing three other jobs, a bit of each, just enough to keep himself out of serious trouble, then he would let them all down in turn. What a way to run a business!

He was the messiest builder I have ever known. He was also a bodger. Walls were not quite straight, doors did not quite fit. When it came to assembling the shower, a two year old could have done better. The result was that I had to re-assemble part of the shower and seal it properly.

The final straw came on the day he was enlarging the hatchway to our loft. He needed a piece of string to hold something and instead of asking us for a cord, he cut half the flex off our junior Hoover and used that instead. Now that Hoover had been in the family since before the second world war, and as any Hoover agent will tell you was one of the best small vacuum cleaners on the market. We had cared for it all these years, and in a matter of seconds, in the hands of this moron, its lifeline had been cut. This Hoover, that had survived the war, fell victim to the total ignorance of this cowboy. That was it, I had had enough. I found this lifeless Hoover when I returned home from work. In a rage I collected his tools together and dumped them outside the front door. I then rang him only to be greeted by his answerphone. Usually they disarm me but my temper was so great I managed to convey a more than adequate message relating to everything from his doubtful parentage to his utter incompetence, adding he was not required anymore.

All I can say to you is beware of builders with fancy associations behind them, carrying albums of their previous work and slick answers to all your questions. They might be cowboys like this one.

BACHELORS

Bachelors are Us Folk, but their way of life is so different that their place in society is almost set aside from the rest of us. Look at the typical night out for our bachelor boy, and you will see how they ignore the feelings of the rest of us completely.

STRIKE FRIDAY FROM MY DIARY

Oh dear, I've even got the date wrong. Actually it's the eleventh, I think. Anyway, I'm fairly certain that it's Saturday. The thing is, yesterday and today seem to have merged with very little snoring space between. It was a farewell party. All very proper and correct, with black ties and those silly cummerbund things that are designed to make your shirt ride half way up your chest.

The programme seemed fairly straight forward: change, meet in the pub, and then go on to the dinner at the Hilton. There were pit-falls and cunning old fate had them well hidden. Seven o'clock saw the six of us dressed as though we were expecting the public to throw us pieces of fish and trying to look inconspicuous in a crowded London pub. Dinner was timed for nine and by eight-thirty we had turned the Red Lyon into the local temple of Bacchus. Everyone bought a round of drinks and I thought that would be it. Wrong: they kept coming. We sang 'For he's a jolly good fellow', a dozen times. The more we supped, the jollier that good fellow became. Tom was sick. Bob tried to kiss the landlord's wife and Harry gave a five pound note to the Salvation Army.

"Is'hunt it about time we where'at leaving?" I heard someone slur and then realised it was me. "One for the road" received short shift and we piled into two taxis and headed for dinner.

The Hilton is always busy Friday night, but not normally noisy. We changed all that. There are few things more noisy than a crowd of drunks trying to be quiet. The food was excellent but then it always is when the taste buds have been swept into the socks by a torrent of booze. I can't remember what I ate, but I do remember some dry Martini, some white wine, some red wine and some brandy. Half past midnight and it was back to my place for a night-cap.

We slumped into the furniture and I tried to loosen my tie before I realised that you can't loosen those elasticised black butterflies. Michael made up a large

bowl of something and handed each of us a glass. It hit me in the back of the throat like a battering ram. "Gordon Bennett," I cried, "what the hell is this?"

"I dunno," he said, "but I wouldn't wash my car with it."

I stared around the room, closed one eye and my ten companions became five again. It was time to go.

Someone had set up an iron foundry in my head. I lay still for a few minutes, waiting for Saint Peter to bring my breakfast. Then, without assistance, I prised open an eyelid. I wiggled my toes and discovered that they were still inside my shoes. Across the room on a hanger and as neat as can be were my jacket and trousers. It seems that was as far as I got undressing. I still had on my socks, shoes, shirt and tie. Getting off the bed was not a problem: I simply rolled over. Getting up from all fours was a different matter, but with the aid of the wardrobe and the bed-side table I managed it. My bathroom is down a flight of stairs and I cursed the architect every step of the way. My intention was to shave, but I didn't recognise the face in the mirror so I settled for the head under the tap treatment. I had a hangover that belonged in the Guinness Book of Records, and over coffee tried to decide between Aspro or Anadin. I finally settled for orange juice and a vitamin pill. I was numb and couldn't tell whether the shower was hot or cold but I did feel a little better afterwards. A raw egg with salt and pepper and a dash of Worcester sauce, another coffee and I was getting healthier by the minute.

Then Michael arrived in his running gear.

"Morning," he said breezily, "been jogging."

"You're nuts," I told him, "you need locking up."

"Trouble with you is that you're growing old."

"Huh," I grunted, "another night like that and I'll be getting dead."

273

"Feeling a bit rough are we?"

"You know, Michael, I cannot imagine why," I said, leaning slightly backwards to get level with my eyeballs.

"Let's go for a beer," he suggested.

The coffee I poured over him soaked his hair, his face and the shoulders of his track suit.

"I take it that means no," he said cheerfully, not appearing to notice.

"Cheerio Michael, see you in a year or two when I feel better." I would have shaken his hand but I was afraid to reach out too far for fear of falling over. Now, let me see, what's on television?

That illustrates the bachelor at play, now lets see him cope with domestics.

THE LAUNDRETTE

There are few things more likely to take the fun out of bachelorhood than a Sunday morning at the Laundromat. That suave, Saturday night Man-About-Town suddenly becomes a lonely, almost pathetic figure, clutching a black rubbish bag full of dirty socks and underwear, and looking about as relaxed as a cat at Crufts Dog Show. However, such visits are essential if you don't have either a washing machine or a rub-a dub-dub lady friend because experience has taught me, at least, that just rinsing the collar and cuffs is all very well when you wear a sweater, but that a tie doesn't hide too many gravy stains. So, off I went this morning.

Standing in front of the machine trying to make some sense out of the operating instructions, I suddenly realised that I had become the centre of attraction. A dozen pairs of eyes had been momentarily diverted from their own slushing and slopping and spinning and were focused on me, the newcomer. Was I self conscious? Does a fish swim?

No matter how carefully you take your dirty linen out of the bag and put it into the machine, by the time the bag is empty you are ankle-deep in at least once-worn unmentionables. Panic is the enemy of composure and by the time I had scooped everything into the machine and closed the door, I was so flummoxed that I couldn't get the money into the slots.

"Need any help?" asked a little old lady glancing up from her knitting.

"Thank you no, I can manage."

Believe me, that was the greatest show of optimism since Custer was going to surround all those Indians. No matter how I pushed and pulled at the coin slide the darn silly thing just refused to engage. Suddenly, the little old lady was at my elbow examining the offending piece of machinery over the top of a pair of metal rimmed spectacles.

"Hmm. You've got the coins in the wrong slots," she said and fiddled around with the end of one of her knitting needles until, with an obvious smile of triumph, she clicked the machine into the first washing cycle.

"There," she said kindly, if a little patronisingly, and went back to the manufacture of what was already a yard long, multi-coloured, something or other.

"Thank you. Thank you very much."

"Oh, that's perfectly all right. I find that we all need a little help occasionally," she said, glancing up from her labours. I felt like the bungling detective to Agatha Christie's Miss Marples, grateful for the assistance but ashamed that I should need it.

The next thirty minutes was easy, but thirty-one minutes and my troubles began again. Mr. Westinghouse's mechanical pride and joy came to a stop. All the lights went out and the indicator showed that the entire washing cycle was complete. The trouble was, my machine was still half full of water.

You have to remember that this was Sunday and there was no attendant on duty. Worse, by this time Miss. Marples had gone, as had everyone else. I was alone. Well, it's facing situations like this that develop strength of character. Initiative, that's what was needed, initiative and common sense. I displayed a great deal of both and opened the machine door. Then I closed it again, quickly, as water began to fill my boots. I sat down and tried to work out plan B.

I was well short of deciding what my next course of action would be when in walked a couple of guys, each carrying a Safeway's shopping bag. They sat alongside and the nearest one turned to me and said,

"Bloody cold out there."

His breath hit me like an updraft from a sewer. I don't know what they had been drinking but if the Russians ever get hold of it they'll have an unapproachable lead in chemical weapons. Anyway, desperation can bring together strange bed-fellows so I thought, "What the heck, maybe they can help."

"Do you know anything about these machines?" I asked, "I can't get the water to drain away."

They glanced at me as if I were something from outer space, then rotated the switches until the machine sprang into action and then set it on final rinse. Simple when you know how!

We look at a bachelors life as an ideal. A path we wish we could have taken, full of excitement and freedom. So what's in the mind of our bachelor boy? What excites him?

276

A BACHELOR'S GREENER GRASS

Marriage? You mean as in, 'I do,' and 'I will,' and 'with all my worldly debts I thee endow?' You do? Well yes, I believe in marriage. After all, without marriage Les Dawson would have only had half an act.

Actually, I envy the married. To love and to be loved and to need and be needed is the greatest happiness there is. Bachelorhood is all very well but it's a horse with no jockey in life's handicap race. Sharing, having someone to reach out to both physically and emotionally: that's what is beautiful and, more often than not, fulfilling. Sharing is caring and comfort and criticism is genuine concern. Oh yes, I envy the married.

Being alone begets loneliness and that self sufficiency which a lot of people admire in us bachelors, is really nothing more than a form of bigotry. 'I'm set in my ways', is an admission of failure. I remember talking to an old friend I hadn't seen for about twenty years. He listened enthralled to my tales of adventure and travel and told me that he wished his life had been half as exciting.

I asked him if he was married and he told me that he was and that he had a teenage family. He told me that, after years of hard work he had reached executive position in his chosen profession, he had a nice house on the edge of town and a small place in the country for the weekends. He told me about his large circle of friends. I shook my head and he saw the sadness in my eyes and understood.

He knew, right at that moment, as I did, that his life had produced far more excitement, adventure and achievement than mine ever could. He had always had a goal, a purpose, an incentive which had eventually made him a success. His was the true happiness, not mine.

EXERCISE

Some of us, in our lives are conned into believing that we can alter our life style by regular exercise. So we go for regular runs or buy ourselves expensive equipment to try and do it the easy way. How much of this equipment gets three to four weeks use and then gathers dust till we give it to a jumble sale? I suspect very few of us persevere with the equipment when the going gets tough.

THE EXERCISER

It happens to most of us at some time during our lives: we get out of bed, shower, shave and start to get dressed. Shirt on, socks and shoes, it doesn't matter which order: at some point comes the stage where you have to fasten your trousers. Even with the deepest of breath the belt has to go one hole looser. You look down and discover that there are buckle marks four holes back and you have only had the belt four months. An exhalation leaves the lower part of your gut on nodding terms with your knees. It's time to do something about the spare tyre which you had previously believed only happened to other people.

The ad columns are full of things like, 'Loose weight overnight'. Come to this clinic or that clinic. Well, you're certain to lose weight because the price will cost you an arm and a leg. So you look further.

I found a beauty: it's a machine on which you sit and push and pull weight ladened ropes. The little picture in the ad makes it look like something designed by a mentally deranged descendent of the Wright brothers. There's a seat, obviously, a rest for each foot with straps to keep the feet in contact and a whole lot of wires, strings, ropes, call them what you will, through which you have to entangle and then dis-entangle yourself. In position, if you ever get that far, you recover your breath and congratulate yourself on the achievement, reach out and take hold of a couple of dangling ropes: then you pull. Nothing happens. You pull again. Still nothing happens. You yank and a sharp pain shoots up your back. You reach for the 'Easy-To-Follow' instructions.

"Hmm," you think, "that seems pretty straightforward."

You pull. Again the machine remains inert. You yank harder this time, but still nothing happens. Angry and frustrated you summon all the strength from your puny and overweight body and heave hard. One of the weights falls off its perch and lands on your trapped foot. It isn't funny and your neighbours, who have overheard your construction-site language will testify to the fact. By this time you've had enough and decide to get off the machine. That's easier said than done. You can't stand up because there's an iron support bar above your head. You can't go forward because there's an iron support bar two inches from your nose. To the left and right there's a tangled mess resembling an unfinished metal cob-web.

Notwithstanding the obstacles you thrust yourself sideways, trip, cut your toe on a piece of the finely finished metalwork, fall forward, hit the carpet face down and consider yourself lucky to have suffered nothing worse than a nosebleed.

279

"I feel better already," you lie to yourself, trying to justify the eighty-five quid you spent on the contraption. You re-dress, feeling that you can come to terms with the extended belt, and head for the local pub.

SUPERMARKETS

Our whole shopping experience is changing for the worse. Going, is the small corner shop with everything you need as the one stop supermarket is bankrupting the small shopkeepers. In this open letter to supermarkets I make a plea for a more customer friendly policy.

SUPERMARKETS TAKE NOTE

Please, do not put your price tags directly over the pull-back flaps on the top of your cans of drinks. Several times I've had to remove one from my mouth which has told me my tongue its only worth forty-five pence.

Please put essential goods in easy reach on your shelves. I once had a word with a supermarket manager about the positioning of goods on his shelves.

"It's marketing psychology," he told me.

I told him that I knew the meaning of the two words but didn't understand their juxtaposition.

"Pardon?" he said.

"Well, I know what marketing is and I know what psychology is. What I don't know is how you justified the two together."

"It's simple," he said, blissfully unaware of the insult to my intelligence.

"You put the goods everybody has to have, on either the top shelf or the bottom shelf. The luxury goods you place on the middle shelves."

"You mean within grabbing distance," I said.

"Well, that's about it, more or less," he said, and turned away thinking that he'd customer-relationed some other sucker, but he hadn't heard the last of me.

"Just a second," I said to the back of his retreating jacket.

I said it with just enough strength of voice to halt him in his tracks and for the close by, heavily laden, trolley pushers to take notice.

"Are you telling me that by placing certain goods in a certain position you can get people to buy them whether they either want them or can afford them?"

He smiled at the trolley pushers, turned his face towards me, snarled and put his arm around me. I felt his finger nails digging into the back of my neck.

"Come with me," he said, we don't want any trouble. We'll discuss whatever grievance we have."

His office was a large desk and a swivel chair in which he sat. The rest of it was a hard back chair on which I sat.

His side of the desk had telephones and filing cabinets and a lot of paper lying around. My side of the desk stared back at his side of the desk and waited for him to say something.

"Now sir," he said. "You have a complaint. What is it?"

"I am just curious to know why psychology is needed to feed the masses?"

———————

There is a whole host of predators after our meagre wealth who make our lives a misery. None more ominous than the funeral director. With his Pow-faced mourning look he will go through your requirements for a simple funeral and with modest manner and sympathetic approach, disguise the fact you are spending a fortune you haven't got to bury a relation you didn't even care too much about. He relies on your embarrassment to stop you from cancelling what you have already agreed, when he tells you the total bill will only be ten thousand pounds.

You feel so sick that you immediately think you will fill the next coffin, killed by the shock. Yes, it isn't cheap to die: at least not for your closest relatives.

Have you ever thought what happens to all those expensive fittings on the coffin when they pass through the curtain of the chapel of rest? Well, there is a team of undertakers the other side who remove them from the coffin before they put the coffin in the furnace. They are used time and time again and the funeral directors charge through the nose for them. Gone are the days when they are buried with you.

Lets put the magnifying glass on another predator competing for our spare cash.

THE DOUBLE GLAZING SALESMAN

Well, it's your fault really. You would talk to that salesman at the county fair. Remember, he wouldn't let you go till you gave him your address and phone number? To overcome that, I always carry fake cards to satisfy their thirst for contacts. (Especially if it is the private address of another double glazing salesman.)

I think they have all been cloned. I really do. On entering the house they immediately pay compliments to you about your decor or choice of furniture, something that they can be sure will put you at ease. You then make your first mistake. You offer him a coffee. You're half hooked. He has you participating in his sales pitch. He will then ask to see the windows that you think need changing. Immediately his tape is out and he is making feverish notes. Back in your living room, he replaces his tape for a calculator which is working overtime. You think he is working out a quote. Wrong, he is calculating how much of his mortgage you are likely to pay off if he can close the deal. This fires him up for the close.

Enthused by his finding he quickly prices up your windows and at this point goes for the closer. It just happens he can squeeze your order into a busy schedule, just before the prices go up at the end of the month. You are so relieved by the two thousand pounds you are going to save, you forget the excessive price he is quoting and can't sign the agreement fast enough. Yes, you have just been caught in a classical sales closer: next month's price increase list that lasts all year.

Remember, the salesman gets between ten and twenty five percent of the money you pay for the windows. So don't feel sorry for him. Some top salesmen earn six figure salaries each year. Check around, you can usually get a much better quote if you look for it. Don't get drawn into their sales pitch. You won't lose out by ignoring their come on's.

Nothing can compare with the car salesman.

THE BARGAIN CENTRE

I was being nagged rotten every evening to lend my car to my daughter, so I decided to go out and see if I could buy her a second hand Fiesta 950 so she would leave me in peace. I chose the Fiesta as it was cheap to service, and low on insurance for young drivers that have recently passed their test. She had passed her test first time and was a reasonably good driver, but impatient at times and drives too fast. A sensible reason not to start with a new car even if you can afford it.

I passed a second-hand car lot every day on the way to work so I decided to stop and look around.

At once a character, looking more like a gangster out of an East end thriller sidled up to me and offered his limited assistance to me with the words; "Have I got a bargain for you mate."

When I had recovered from this attack on my sensibility he urged me forward till I was standing in front of an elderly Mercedes with more ripples on its panels than a lake in a force eight gale.

"Sorry," I said, "I'm looking for a Ford Fiesta 950 for my daughter."

"Good choice," he replied, "I have three, but this one is the best."

From what I saw it looked the part, clean inside and out and apparently low mileage: if that could be believed.

"Belonged to an old couple. Only went out once a month." (Now where have I heard that before?)

"What's your best price for that car?" I asked.

"We keep our prices low to sell cars," he said, "what you see is our best price."

"Even for cash?"

He seemed to be taken aback. "We don't sell cars for cash, only on the knock." (A quaint term for hire purchase.)

I left disappointed till today, when a friend of mine told me he bought a car from the same dealer, on the knock and when it ceased to work, he asked the dealer to collect it and repair it under warrantee. They refused. He stopped paying and it was repossessed.

I thought to myself, 'that's a crafty way of getting deposits and one or two payments before repossess the car, repair it and sell it again'. Two months later the same car was in the news. The next sucker had found out it was a ringer. (Built from two crashed cars.)

Never trust a second hand car salesman: always get advice.

With new car salesmen you have other problems. Every car salesman has a quota to sell and at certain times of the year that can be very difficult to meet. At that time he is most pliable and will negotiate up to fifteen percent discount and/or an extras deal. So don't give up, find a salesman that is pliable and go for it.

TELEVISION

Television could have been the greatest educational instrument of this century. Instead the commercial channels have pandered to the baser instincts of the human being and its lust for sex and violence, and shamefully side-stepped the vocational opportunity to educate and stimulate. This is a sweeping statement and it is not wholly true as there are small pockets of education and innovation, but not nearly enough.

Sadly to compete for audience the BBC have gone the same way, losing the great battle to educate.

Television is inundated with chat shows, most of which are so self gratifying to the celebrities you think, 'this is a set up'. Oscar award ceremonies must go down as the biggest switch off on television. Don't the profession love giving each other Oscars? It's amazing, you see the same people show after show, either giving or receiving a lump of glass or cast of metal. There must be a whole industry out there working twenty-four hours a day to produce these awards.

Then there is the inevitable quiz show. Some with audience, some celebrity participation. At first these were quite entertaining, but now they have become so repetitive they are boring. It is a big switch off.

Quite often the advertisements are better than the programme. Those chimpanzees have a large following, as does the dog with the toilet paper. Lets take a look at the influence of advertising on the sub-conscious.

THE WRONG BED

I welcome bed-time because it's the time when the world goes away.

There are no threateningly phrased letters from the bank manager. No tap on the shoulder from the building society. The price of tomatoes has gone down and petrol is something you don't have to worry about because you're being transported on a cloud which needs no fuel other than your dreams.

You open the batting for England; score the winning goal in the Cup Final; you stand on the top of Everest, having got there single-handed and without an oxygen-mask; You've sailed round the world twice: non-stop; you've spoken to the leaders of the world and received the Nobel Peace Prize. BANG!

Halfway through the night a trip to the lavatory becomes necessary.

Back into bed, punching pillows into some form of gentleness upon which we lay our head. Drift into sleep: but this time the dreams are fired by the curry and onions you haven't yet digested.

You're out for a duck on the village green. You're only the ball-boy at a soccer match played between a couple of third eleven's. Everest becomes a sand castle which is kicked in your face. The world around which you have sailed your boats becomes the rubber duck in the bath-tub: and all those world leaders you met and the Nobel Prize you won are landlords and bookmakers who smile, shake your hand and say, "Thank you."

When you awake, you find you slept the second time around on the wrong sofa. It was not a Multi-York!!

Now for the weather forecast. High pressure is bringing rain storms and thunder over much of the country with snow over high ground.

So you might as well stay in bed and dream away.

WHAT DEMOCRACY

Politicians spare no energy to inform us we live in a democracy. The media constantly uphold the democratic flag, but are we a true democracy or a fraud?

To understand democracy let us first enlighten ourselves with the meaning of the word from our dictionary. It says in my learned book; Democracy: 'A system of government by the whole population through elected representatives'.

From this brief description, the meaning of democracy is clear. That is to say we elect representatives to present our general views to parliament, and a consensus of representation that holds the majority on any given issue wins the vote. This should give us a popular decision making mechanism to compliment the majority view on any subject.

Alas, party politics puts paid to that fanciful notion and combined with the civil service blurs the subject to be reviewed to such an extent that no one quite knows what has been eventually achieved. That is the way politicians can do what they like at the expense of our democratic rights.

Lets take a look at so-called democracy in action. Over a year ago the government announced a public enquiry into terminal five at Heathrow airport to be held at the Ramada hotel. It was scheduled to last for two years.

The lobbyists thought they had won a resounding victory. Wrong. Although the government announced an enquiry into terminal five to outwardly show a democratic process in action, cynically the main decisions for terminal five had already been made, and only fine tuning to the scheme was up for discussion and alteration. In this way the pressure groups have been conned into believing they were participating in a democratic process.

When the going got tough before the enquiry the government arranged that the British Airport Authority should announce that the need for a third runway was no longer essential. This, far from being final, was a necessary move to push through terminal five and I will give you a level bet that seven years from terminal five opening the subject of a third runway will be brought forward and land us with another democratic fraud.

How do I know a decision has been made to build terminal five on the West side of the airport? Simple; for the last two years they have been emptying the sewage site which is the location of terminal five. A tube station has already been located under this site and only needs outfitting.

British Airways have, for the past six months, been building Prospect Park next to the old sewage plant which will be their new headquarters. This is to have underground access to terminal five under the A4. Terminal five is to service British Airways passengers only.

So why this pathetic fraud? Why can't the government have the guts to say we need more facility at Heathrow for the future; apologise for the inconvenience this will cause to some local residents, and use the money spent on the enquiry to help those affected? This would give them far more praise as the country is in general, supporting terminal five.

This half lying, half hidden system the civil service uses to get its way is totally discredited and a symbol of a secretive society run by un-elected bureaucrats. It is known that Britain is the most secretive country in the world today. They seem to drop democracy when democracy can't be trusted to assist their view.

Now lets examine whether Europe will deliver the lost democracy we desire. When Britain voted to enter Europe by referendum a simple question was asked. Do we want to be part of an expanding European market with two-hundred and eighty million customers or be left out in increasing isolation? This was democracy at work, and it was a simple decision: in or out. At least that is what it seemed. However, like everything else presented to us to decide upon, the simple question was only the tip of the iceberg. What was under the surface was dangerous for our sovereignty and wholly against the interests of Britain. We were sold a pup by the Right hon. Edward Heath who surely knew the whole story.

I, for one, voted to go in and now realise it was the worst vote I have ever cast and I know millions of fellow countrymen feel the same. We are not alone, so do millions of disenchanted Europeans.

You see, we thought we voted for a free trade, open gate European policy and that was all. A large market without restrictions on goods or money crossing the borders, just controlled enough to see fair competition between member states. If the EU was just that then the majority of people in Europe and in Britain would still support it.

Instead the politicians and Eurocrats have turned it into an inefficient third tier of government that overrules our sovereign parliament and national interests. It spends our money like water and is controlled by non elected Eurocrats directed mainly by France and Germany. This control is to the detriment of all ordinary people in the participating countries.

Daily, we seem to have our court decisions overturned by the European Court Of Justice. In doing so, they interfere with our internal system of justice that has been built up on precedent over many years. A system that built upon the Magna Carta. This European court's ill-considered judgements will end up costing the tax payers of Britain and indeed Europe, money they do not possess; if it is allowed to continue along the lines it has set itself.

I am not arguing whether their decisions are right or wrong but whether the matters should be allowed to be judged outside our jurisdiction and further allowed to set precedents for all grievances before them. If this is to continue it will open the flood gates for massive and uncontrollable claims. Us Folk, in the end, have to find the money to pay these bills, not the EU or the state. We have no say in the decision so why should we be liable for their unrepresentative decisions?

An example shows clearly how this undemocratic court, outside our jurisdiction, is running rough-shod over our sovereign courts who seem powerless to halt their follies. There is the case of a teacher who decided to have a sex change and was consequently, in my opinion, rightly sacked. The court made a grave error to interfere in our internal affairs when the consequence of the judgement would influence the minds of the children in contact with that teacher. This most important consideration, did not seem to be a matter of importance to the Judges. Once again our democratic right to make our own judgements have been thwarted by this monster.

Suddenly, the unthinkable is being voiced by thousands of people in Britain and also championed by the press and even in parliament. Us Folk are fed up with the myth of EU unity and democracy. Should Britain come out of this over rated straight jacket that will suffocate its members if they wait and hope?

The weight of issues against continued membership is so great: the silly judgements metered out by the European Courts of Justice, the farcical collapse of the ERM, the stupidity of the relentless drive towards a single currency in lemming like style. The madness of a single parliament that lays redundant centuries of our established power and hands it to an undemocratic assembly in true Marxist style. The destruction of our, once proud, fishing industry. The sudden realisation that we have already given our last vestige of democracy to Brussels and a much larger un-democratic system. The beef crisis, escalated by the EU into a vendetta against Britain to bring it into line over the single currency and the social chapter: to name but a few.

The main reason Edward Heath gave us for joining the European community was simply that it was a large market and we were suffering from a declining economy.

So what have twenty-three years of membership done to prove Edward Heath's promise of a better future inside Europe? Nothing. Quite the reverse has happened. Before we entered the EU we were running a modest surplus with Europe. In twenty-three years of being a member the surplus has turned into a staggering deficit of one-hundred billion pounds, only covered by an energetic sales campaign by industry in the rest of the world showing a healthy surplus. We were assured our future lay with Europe. I, for one, feel betrayed. Don't you?

Worse, the collapse of the ERM has been estimated, by a team at Bradford University, to have cost us, as tax payers, a further seventy billion pounds. Add to this the one-hundred billion pounds we have handed to Brussels for our contribution. Then their is the extra cost of food to each family of four, estimated, at one-thousand pounds a year per family to prop up the discredited agricultural support system, CAP. It is clear to see how easily, if it goes on this way, they can bankrupt us all. Add to all that the latest treasury report. It predicts a bleak future for Britain if it joins the single currency. It says Britain will become a third world nation by 2015.

The reason that Britain is doing better than its partners in the EU is because we came out of the ERM, and stayed out of the social chapter. Despite Edward Heath's statement that world and Commonwealth trade was falling it has held up well and increased. We now sell fifty-six percent of our goods outside the EU with an impressive increase to the Middle and far East and the old Commonwealth.

What we must ask ourselves is can we afford to stay in a loss making community that is run on undemocratic principles akin to Marxist teaching, where the decisions of policy are drafted by civil servants and the courts run by un-elected judiciary, all of which regularly dip their hands in our pocket and extract our hard earned cash from our over-taxed savings. Can we indeed continue to find the taxes to cover our excessive payment to Europe for them to squander? The lack of financial control, leading to the ERM disaster, the unchecked fraud inside CAP in countries like Italy and Spain, where syndicates like the Mafia skim the support policy for all it's worth, in most cases without detection. Then the unpredictable policy of single currency which in turn will lead to a single parliament. These useless policies it appears are so unpopular that only a handful of politicians and a legion of empire building Eurocrats in the civil service support them. Now is the time to ask the question seriously. Are we better off out than in?

The evidence weighs heavily in favour of coming out. We must have a referendum now to debate this important decision. We cannot leave it to the politicians as they benefit from its gravy train; therefore they will not represent our views in parliament. Their record on this issue is shameful.

Home owners, caught in the price trap of negative equity have the collapse of the ERM to thank for their misery. Firms and the public, that's Us Folk, have paid a high interest rate because of the German manipulation of the interest rates to ease the burden of their reunification programme for East Germany.

Many businesses, who used to be in favour of the EU, would now vote to come out as the twenty-thousand directives from the EU bureaucrats have made their life unbearable and constantly threatens competitiveness.

Surveys prove small business is being suffocated by EU regulations. Sixty percent have complained that directives have increased cost.

The social chapter has caused mass unemployment in Europe. Britain alone opted out and warned it would do just that. How long can we maintain our stand with Germany and France gunning for us?

Business in Britain wants out. The people of Britain want out. Major conceded that when he answered a question on the referendum recently. So why, tell us why, do all the main parties maintain a pro-European stance, leaving us with no party to adopt our preference? Do they not listen to us or is it more rewarding to chase a dead duck for its inheritance?

Britain must come out of Europe now, before it clamps us fully into its system and brings us down. This matter is far too vital to our future happiness to ignore.

ADVOCATE COW'S ADDRESS TO THE HOUSE OF COMMONS

Madam speaker, honourable members. On this unusual occasion, I am standing before you to put my members case for caution against knee-jerk reaction to calls for a mass slaughter of my members. The truth is that no scientist knows the source of BSE (Bovine Spongiform Encephalopathy).

BSE was officially recognised in 1986. Since then the Ministry of Agriculture, Fisheries and Food have claimed it was a new disease which it was not. It had clearly been around for some time as the veterinary profession have confirmed.

However, the ministry, in its typical clumsy manner have tripped up over their own tongues each time they opened their excuse exits. They don't know the cause neither do our scientists in America Europe and elsewhere. So they started a speculative answer by blaming cattle feed with our remains in it.

By claiming it was a new disease MAFF (Ministry of Agriculture, Food and Fisheries) was under considerable pressure to find an answer, so they conceived a Scientist's educated guess that the scrapie agent was passed to my members through under-processed feed.

This started the panic theory that scrapie from sheep somehow had jumped the species barrier and infected cows. If it could jump barriers, could it jump to the eaters of beef or its products? Therefore the best theory was presented to the press without thought of its probable consequence.

It was then, in 1989 Kieth Meldrum, the chief veterinary officer, stated the epidemic was under control and would soon scale down over the next few years.

It didn't, as the theory was ill founded and therefore the panic factor started to rise. Scientists, one after the other, declined to eat beef. Still MAFF fumbled and sang but with no conviction to assure the panic factor they knew anything new.

Evidence is however available from America that BSE cannot jump species. This has been proved by professor Marsh and Professor Caughey, they found scrapie doesn't cause BSE in cattle.

No specific research is sure to produce the answer, but two seem to be front runners; the first is the study of the formation of natural protein in the body which changes its form naturally, without external agents. Research is in its early stages to isolate the causes of this mutation.

The second front runner is the use of phosmet treated feeds which were used in Britain in particularly high levels and follow the infection pattern in dairy cattle. The feed was used mainly for dairy herds which supports the evidence of infection.

MAFF continues to mis-handle the PR side of their duties and the minister at the head of the department, Douglas Hogg, has fumbled his way round Europe in my opinion, doing more harm than good.

Ten deaths have occurred in as many years from Creutzfeldt-Jacob disease. In one year alone one-hundred thousand humans die from lung cancer, yet so far their is no full cure for cancer. Did we cull them? Do we even panic over this situation? No, we try to find a cure.

However, information has come to light that the main cause of lung cancer is not cigarette smoking as widely claimed by government but Diesel fumes inhaled by us all on the roads. This has been known by government since the sixties but they have failed to pass on the result of two reports. Furthermore they have tried to promote diesel as a clean fuel.

Diesel fumes could be the cause of a death rate of major concern. So why the panic over a new disease with a very low fatal rate?

It is my opinion the panic button was purposely pressed by the ruling group in Europe from Germany and their bureaucratic counterparts in the EU. I think they cynically believed they could use the unfortunate position Britain found itself in to force us into line over majority voting, single currency, and federalism.

The German foreign minister, Klaus Kinkel, said as much to the press in April 96; "Solidarity is not a one-way street, the British now expect solidarity from us in connection with BSE. That's legitimate. But in return we can demand solidarity from the British in the Turin inter-governmental conference on extending European integration". This means they want Britain to drop their veto power for a majority voting system, giving greater power to the EU parliament.

So Europe's concern over BSE is false. They are using the uncertain cause of the disease to bring Britain into line with their Marxist influenced policies: Europe must stand condemned for insisting on the mass murder of my members for political gain, that has nothing to do with solving BSE.

Most countries in Europe have experienced the disease. Why aren't their herds being slaughtered at random? The reason is that it is pointless murder.

I accuse Europe of demanding mass murder of my members without just reason.

Now I must turn to the motives of the honourable members. I have always believed Britain to be a caring country that took pride in its National Health Service. I have seen no evidence of mass genocide amongst cancer sufferers. They might isolate patients with dangerous diseases but they don't cull them.

Even with killer diseases like Aids, which so far has no cure, sufferers are treated with kindness and understanding. So why do you think you have the right to order mass extermination of my members as a sop to Europe when it is clear Europe is using this unfortunate situation for their own gain?

You are offering my members lives in return for no firm guarantee and you won't get one. My members have the right to the same compassion, the same understanding, and the same concern as Aids or cancer sufferers.

Culling my members will solve none of your problems including Europe. It will just be random murder. There is not one shred of scientific proof a mass cull will have any lasting benefit in curtailing this dreadful disease.

You should be backing serious attempts to come to an understanding of the disease. A vet has nearly perfected a simple test to find out if my members have contracted the disease. He needs funding to reach his target. This is the type of project worth your attention.

Instead you muddle along from day to day and let Europe walk all over you.

Let's just look at a few of the unacceptable policies Europe is trying to force on you. British courts can now be overruled by the European Courts of Justice. In this respect it can also overrule the sovereign power of parliament.

It has brought you great financial lose through the ERM. You escaped only to be told you must be ready for ERM control to bring you to a single currency by 1999. If you vote for that it'll put you back into a strait-jacket and ruin Britain.

Twenty thousand directives from the Brussels bureaucrats have left industry reeling from interference, some so ridiculous they are laughable. It has also increased the cost of products.

The Common Agricultural Policy is rife with fraud from strong criminal organisations like P2 and the Mafia and is estimated to cost each family of four an extra one-thousand pounds per year on their food bill; nothing is done to reverse it.

Homeowners suffered from negative equity and businesses from high interest rates because the pound was tied to the Deutschmark and Germany kept interest rates high to help pay for the reunification of East Germany. By 'Black Wednesday' Britain had squandered seventeen billion pounds of reserves to keep themselves in the ERM. It failed and we left; immediately the pound recovered and today your

prospects are better in Britain than all other European countries. Many homeowners and businessmen alike lost everything because the Bank of England was so slow to react.

Britain, until now, has resisted attempts to join the social chapter, the very legislation that is crippling Europe's industries and causing Europe's highest recorded unemployment figures since the thirties. Britain has not joined the Social Chapter and has maintained low unemployment but how long will this last? Europe is now imposing the same policy on you through the health and safety agenda so your freedom is short lived.

Brussels is trying to rubbish your double-decker busses in a cynical attempt to gain some of your market in the middle and far East.

They want to take our sovereignty away through, first the single currency and then the single parliament. Effectively this power will be able to override parliament and our sovereignty. You will be puppets to a remote parliament uncontrolled by your people.

For Britain to abandon its currency then its parliamentary power would be abdication of responsibility by this house: tantamount to treason.

They have ruined your fishing industry and handed it to Spain; yet Spanish trawlers are allowed to register in this country and therefore count as part of your greatly reduced quotas.

I could go on for a week about the damage membership of Europe has done to this country but time does not permit.

I end by asking you this question: "Considering what Europe has done to Britain in twenty three years of myth about where our best interest lie - Who is the mad cow, Mr. Prime Minister?"

THE SEASONS

The snow has gone, leaving the common a mixture of soggy brown mud and damp uninspiring greenery. The stark, hardness of January and February are forgotten. Heavy overcoats are back in the wardrobes. Smiles are back on the faces and people wave at each other in the early spring sunshine. Snowdrops, our first signal of spring, are saying goodbye as the sharp tips of daffodils and the crocus offer their incomparable promise. There will be, shortly and suddenly, a splendid blaze of colour: blues and yellows and greens and purples and reds. That great mistress of nature, Spring, is donning her best yearly wardrobe to tempt and titillate. Being the great mistress she is, she knows we will respond.

She guarantees that when she has the trees of her court stretch, shake their branches and begin to put on those little pieces of nature's jewellery, the buds and flowers, she will have captivated, teased and brought us to submission and thankfulness. The mistress of nature is and always will be, the promise of tomorrow. She is not a jealous creature mistress of Spring, she knows her affair with us is brief, all too brief. She knows that her fashions will, all too quickly, be replaced by the glory of summer. But our mistress of Spring does not walk away, she backs off gently, holding out her hand at the end of April and the start of May.

Summer is beauty, glory and magnificence. It's a time of warmth and love and friendship. It's a time when little boys play games on the common without wearing rubber boots. It's a time when those same small boys fall and roll over without the fear of mother's wrath because they have brought home an
impossible washing problem. Summer is a time when dogs can sniff and find that bone they buried beneath the hard

ground a couple of months before. Summer is a time for light music and dancing and holding hands and laughing and being happy. Unfortunately, Summer, like Spring, is all too short. With the sparkle in our eyes and the laughter in our hearts still lingering, we turn and we bow and we raise our hands in farewell to Summer as nature plays out it's third act in it's annual play upon our emotions.

The leaves start to fall off the trees, but not before giving us a picture of Autumn colours that stun us with their beauty. The branches sag, and I swear that every Autumn I see a tear in the eye of every tree, in every flower, in every living creature. It is, truly, a time of sadness. It is mother nature's wisdom which has created the beauty of life: it's coldness, it's promise, it's beauty and its sadness. Let that good lady not be put down. She has given us, to you and to me, the seasons. I hope that you can thank her as much as I do as I turn to face another cold and icy Winter.

With all the disappointments of life's expectancy, nature and laughter combine to make our life worth living.

I'll drink to that.

No mind is thoroughly well organised that is deficient in a sense of humour.

Samual Taylor Coleridge   1792-1834.

Total absence of humour renders life
impossible.

Sidonie Gabrielle Colette. 1873-1954.

The pain passes but the beauty remains.

Pierre Auguste Renoir. 1841-1919.
Explaining why he still painted when his hands
were twisted by arthritis.

Laughter is the best medicine.

NOTES

NOTES

NOTES

NOTES